"What's bothering you?" Kiki asked. But as close as she was to him, she could feel his body's reaction to hers.

"You are," he said, and his breath whispered across her mouth.

She parted her lips, breathing him in before releasing a shaky, wistful sigh. "Fletcher..." She couldn't remember the last time she'd been this attracted to someone. And they hadn't even kissed.

She stretched up a bit and brushed her mouth across his. Heat swept through her body.

"This is a bad idea," Fletcher murmured.

"What?" she asked, playing coy.

"I can't afford any distractions right now, not with this investigation, and my cover..." But then he kissed her back, as she'd kissed him, just brushing his mouth across hers before pulling back.

"What's the distraction?" she asked.

"You are," he repeated. "So damn distracting..." And he kissed her again.

Dear Reader,

I am thrilled and honored to be part of **The Coltons of Owl Creek** continuity series. My book *Colton's Dangerous Cover* is the second in the series, with things definitely heating up in Owl Creek between Detective Fletcher Colton and DJ Kiki Shelton. But of course, their "relationship" is just a cover to catch a serial attacker. Or is it?

I loved writing this book. While I've written about a lot of officers of the law over the years, this is my first time writing about a DJ. This is probably because I have no musical ability myself. Per my elementary school music teacher, I am definitely tone-deaf. When tested on which musical instrument I should play, I was told, "No. Just no." While I can't tell which note is which, I do love music and dancing, so writing Kiki's character was a joy.

I also enjoyed writing about the puppy she's fostering for Crosswinds Training. Fancy, the little shepherd mix, reminded me so much of the shepherd-mix dogs my family had while I was growing up. They were all loving, loyal, protective and so very smart.

And as always, Colton books are about family. Those sibling and cousin connections I know so well because I have so many of both.

Hopefully you'll enjoy reading my contribution to the continuity as much as I enjoyed writing it.

Happy reading!

Lisa Childs

COLTON'S DANGEROUS COVER

Lisa Childs

Special thanks and acknowledgment are given to **Lisa Childs** for her contribution to **The Coltons of Owl Creek** miniseries.

HARLEQUIN®
ROMANTIC SUSPENSE™

Recycling programs
for this product may
not exist in your area.

ISBN-13: 978-1-335-59394-8

Colton's Dangerous Cover

Copyright © 2024 by Harlequin Enterprises ULC

For questions and comments about the quality of this book, please contact us at CustomerService@Harlequin.com.

Harlequin Enterprises ULC
22 Adelaide St. West, 41st Floor
Toronto, Ontario M5H 4E3, Canada
www.Harlequin.com

Printed in U.S.A.

New York Times and *USA TODAY* bestselling, award-winning author **Lisa Childs** has written more than eighty-five novels. Published in twenty countries, she's also appeared on the *Publishers Weekly*, Barnes & Noble and Nielsen Top 100 bestseller lists. Lisa writes contemporary romance, romantic suspense, paranormal and women's fiction. She's a wife, mom, bonus mom, avid reader and less avid runner. Readers can reach her through Facebook or her website, lisachilds.com.

Visit the Author Profile page at Harlequin.com for more titles.

With great appreciation for the talented authors also contributing to this Colton continuity—it's been an honor and a pleasure!

Chapter 1

The music was loud, even in the alley. Pulsating. Throbbing. It was alive. Like the rage burning inside the Slasher.

After the third assault a couple of years ago, that was what the media had named the attacker: *The Slasher*.

The Slasher smiled, enjoying the name and the attention. That attention was finally being paid for the right reason. For the power. Not the weakness. *This* was all about taking power back, about taking it away from them.

He would have found the note by now. The invitation for this tryst in the alley. He wouldn't know for certain who'd left it for him, but he would think he was going to get lucky. He had no idea...

A door creaked open, letting some light and louder music seep into the alley. "Hello?" a man's voice called out. "Are you out here?"

Still deep in the shadows, the Slasher called out in a husky whisper, "Over here..."

The guy chuckled, low in his throat, and stumbled away from the door, letting it click closed behind him. Darkness enveloped the area again, but for a thin sliver of moonlight slicing between the tall buildings on either side of the alley.

That thin sliver provided just enough light for the Slasher to see the victim, and for there to be a glint off the sharp blade as the Slasher swung the knife toward the head of the next victim.

Fletcher Colton was dealing with his last case with Salt Lake City PD before he would head home to Owl Creek, Idaho. It was another slasher case. He hoped this job wouldn't cause him to postpone his start date for the position he'd accepted with Owl Creek PD as lead detective.

This case was getting a little personal for him. This was the second time the Slasher had struck in Salt Lake City. Fletcher hadn't worked the first case; he'd already been working a homicide, which had taken priority over an assault. So far, the Slasher hadn't killed anyone.

But the wounds across the victim's face and chest were so deep that the man was going to have to spend some time in the hospital while they healed to make sure they didn't get infected. These wounds were even deeper than the ones the last victim had received. The violence seemed to be escalating.

So it was just a matter of time before someone died, Fletcher thought. And even if they didn't, the Slasher's victims were going to be scarred for life—physically and mentally as well. The Slasher had to be stopped. These two cases in Salt Lake weren't the only assaults. Over the past few years, there had been random attacks outside nightclubs in LA and Vegas. And now Salt Lake City. The randomness made it impossible to figure out where the Slasher would strike next.

Fletcher wanted to make sure that it was nowhere. He'd already interviewed the victim at the hospital. Now he was at the scene, watching as the techs collected evidence. Or at least he hoped they were collecting something that could be used as evidence. Lights had been set up in the alley so that nothing would be missed. The light illuminated the spatters and pools of blood from the attack that had been violent and vicious.

And somehow personal...

But the victim had no connection with the last one. At least none this victim, Eric Holt, was aware of. Fletcher couldn't find any association to the victims in the other states.

What the hell was the motive?

Maybe there wasn't one.

Was this just some psycho who randomly picked victims to disfigure?

"Not much here, Detective Colton," one of the techs said. "Not even footprints, and given the amount of blood, I would have expected to find something."

Fletcher pushed a hand through his dark hair, which probably needed a cut, like usual, and sighed. "The victim wasn't able to give us any useful info either. Everything happened so fast. He couldn't even tell if it was a man or a woman who attacked him." The guy had been vague about all the details, but then he was pretty drunk—with a blood alcohol level that was twice the legal limit.

That was the one thing all the victims had had in common. They'd been drinking. A lot. This guy had been at his bachelor party. So had one of the other victims...

But the others had just been at the club as far as Fletcher knew. He had to find something else. Another lead. "I'm going inside to do some interviews," he told the tech. "Let me know if you find any—"

His cell rang, and he pulled it out of his jacket pocket. The contact information read *Uncle Buck*. In the middle of interviews, he would have ignored it...if not for what had happened recently with his sister Ruby, for how close they had come to losing her forever. But that case had been closed and the deranged guy was locked up. She should be safe, especially with Sebastian Cross so determined to make sure she and their unborn child stayed out of harm's way.

Still, Fletcher was concerned enough that he swiped to accept the call. "Uncle Buck, what is it? I'm at a crime—"

"It's your dad, Fletcher. He's had another stroke. It doesn't look good. He's been life-flighted to Boise Medical. You need to get there as soon as you can."

Fletcher cursed. His relationship with his dad was complicated, but Robert Colton was still his dad. Fletcher loved him even though he got frustrated with him, like he was now. "After the last stroke, he was supposed to quit the drinking and smoking..."

And whatever the hell else he'd been doing that he shouldn't have been doing, that he wouldn't have been doing if he'd cared about anyone but himself.

"Fletcher, it's too late for all of that now," Buck said, his voice gruff with emotion.

A twinge of guilt struck Fletcher. He shouldn't have been thinking about that, let alone voicing his thoughts aloud. He shouldn't have been thinking about anything but his dad's health and about his family. Buck's relationship with his brother hadn't always been the easiest either, but they were brothers. If his dad didn't recover from this stroke like his last one, it wasn't going to be easy for anyone to handle, especially not Fletcher's mother.

"I'll be there as soon as I can," Fletcher assured his uncle.

He had already turned in his resignation to leave Salt Lake City PD for Owl Creek. Someone else would have to take over this case. Someone else would have to catch the Slasher before anyone else got hurt.

Kiki Shelton's hand shook as she scrolled through the messages and posts popping up on the screen of her cell phone. *Oh, no...*

Not another one...

She had to call, had to make sure everyone she knew was all right. She glanced toward the closed door off the kitchen that was dark but for the dim glow of the under-cabinet lighting. Soft snores emanated from behind that door. Her grandfather had gone to bed a while ago, but he was a light sleeper, especially when they were fostering a puppy for Crosswinds.

Fancy was a little two-month-old shepherd mix with tan fur everywhere but her muzzle, which was as black as Kiki's hair. Except for her deep auburn tips. The puppy bounced around Kiki's bare legs, excited that someone else was awake at this hour. Kiki wanted the two of them to be the only ones, so she opened the patio door and stepped onto the deck attached to the back of the cottage.

She didn't want her grandfather to overhear her talking on the phone. He already worried about her too much. He didn't need to know that there had been another attack. In addition to the texts and calls sent directly to her, news of the slashing had also popped up on all her social media accounts.

Thank God Jim Shelton still refused to pay attention to any of them. But he would probably catch it on the news. He never failed to watch the network broadcasts every morning and every night, flipping from channel to channel to get different takes on the same story.

There was only one take on this one. There was a maniac brutally attacking people.

Concerned that someone else had been hurt, she made the call she'd been anxious to make.

"Kiki!" the male voice cracked with the exclamation of her name.

"Are you okay?" she asked Troy. He was usually her assistant, but she'd loaned him out to another DJ since she hadn't had a gig this weekend.

He'd been there. In Salt Lake City. At that very club where the attack had happened…

"It's messed up, Kiki," he said. "I stepped outside to smoke and saw the guy lying there…"

"I'm so sorry, Troy," she said, her stomach churning over the thought of what her friend had found, had seen. And that poor man. "That's horrible. Are you okay? Is he?"

"Yeah, I'm okay. It was way worse for him, but I think he'll live. But it was so bad…" His voice cracked again, and she could hear his shudder through the home. "It's just messed up, Kiki…" He slurred a bit; maybe he'd had something to drink or maybe he was just tired.

It was late. But Kiki was used to staying up late; so was Troy. "You need to get some rest," she suggested.

"Every time I close my eyes I see him there, all cut up and bleeding…" She heard the shudder again.

"Take some time off for a while," she said.

"If I'm not working, I'll just keep thinking about it…"

"Then join me early in Owl Creek," she said. She had some gigs set up for them in the area in a few weeks. "It's safe here. Nothing much happens."

She wouldn't tell him about what had happened at Crosswinds—how she could have lost a good friend. But that criminal had been caught, so Owl Creek was safe again.

Like it had always been…

Kiki's safe haven. After she'd lost her parents in a horrific car accident when she was six, she had come to live with her grandfather along the shore of Blackbird Lake. She leaned on the deck railing and stared out at the surface of the lake, which reflected the night sky and the stars twinkling in it along with the big crescent moon.

It was beautiful here and so quiet, just cicadas chirping in the night as fireflies flitted around like sparks, appearing and disappearing. Fancy tore around the yard, chasing after them, her little teeth snapping as she tried to capture them in her mouth. But it was still quiet, despite the antics of the puppy.

So quiet and so beautiful that it always seemed to recharge Kiki, especially after a long winter and spring of playing clubs in LA and San Francisco and Salt Lake City. But the money she was saving and the reputation she was building was worth all the hard work.

She should have been working the club in Salt Lake this weekend, but she'd wanted to stick around Owl Creek to make sure Ruby was okay and that her grandfather could handle the new puppy. Every time she came home, it seemed like he'd aged while she was gone. And she didn't want him being alone so often, even though he insisted he was as spry as he ever was. And the truth was, he probably preferred to be alone. Either working with puppies from Crosswinds, at his tackle shop or his favorite place, out on his boat on the water, fishing.

"You sure, Kiki?"

She had pretty much forgotten Troy was still on the line. "What?"

"You sure it's safe there?"

She thought of what Ruby Colton had just gone

through. But that was over now. "Yes, it's safe here, Troy. Come to Owl Creek."

But as she clicked off the cell, a strange shiver chased down her spine. Maybe it was just the night breeze. Maybe it was foreboding. After what had happened with Ruby, was Owl Creek as safe as Kiki had always believed it was?

Or maybe that just proved that something bad could happen anywhere…

Chapter 2

The past week had passed in a blur of hospital vigils and now this: the funeral.

Fletcher's dad hadn't survived this stroke like he had the last one. After days in a coma, Robert Colton's body had given up the fight. He'd slipped silently away from them.

"Are you sure you don't want to say anything?" Fletcher's older brother asked him.

He shook his head, uncertain what he could say about his father. Sure, he'd loved him, but he'd also sometimes wondered how well he'd really known him. Robert Colton had spent more time at work than with his family.

"No, Chase," Fletcher said. His older brother, who'd worked with his dad at Colton Properties, knew their father far better than Fletcher had. Fletcher just wanted to make sure that Mom was all right and made it through this day. To find her, he moved through the crowd of family and friends and Owl Creek residents who'd gathered in the funeral parlor to mourn or at least to support the mourners.

Every one of his siblings had someone standing beside them, offering their condolences and probably memories of his father. He'd heard his share already, during the hospital vigils, and at the visitation the night before. He really just wanted this to be over, for his sake, and for his mom's.

Over the past week Jenny Colton had been strong and loving, as she always was, comforting her *kids* instead of letting them comfort her. Maybe that was because she was a nurse and was just used to taking care of others. Maybe that was just because she was an amazing person.

She'd raised not just her own six kids pretty much on her own while Dad had worked crazy long hours, but she'd also helped Uncle Buck raise his four kids after Aunt Jessie, Mom's twin, had abandoned her husband and family. They were all adults now, but Jenny Colton still always put them first, before herself.

But she always made time to take care of her physical health. Fit and active, the only indication of her age were the streaks of gray in her short, dark blond hair. Fletcher breathed a little sigh of relief that she was all right, that she was healthy.

But how was she doing emotionally?

It had been a long week for him. He couldn't imagine how it had felt for her. He found her with Ruby and Sebastian, which he totally understood after they could have lost Ruby. Instead, they'd lost Dad.

Mom wasn't the only one standing near them. An older man with thick white hair, Jim Shelton, stood beside Sebastian. He'd been running a bait and fishing business on Blackbird Lake for as long as Fletcher could remember. And the woman standing next to him looked nothing like his little orphaned granddaughter who'd come to live with him so long ago.

Kiki Shelton, with beautiful, thick black hair and ample curves, had certainly grown up over the past twenty years. She seemed to get more beautiful every time Fletcher saw her, but that hadn't been very often recently. He'd been working his way to detective in Salt Lake City, and she'd been working clubs in LA and Vegas and San Francisco. She'd even worked some in Salt Lake City. Ruby had let him know a few times when Kiki was DJing, but going to a club, with the noise and the crowds, wasn't his idea of a good time. At least on the few times he had ventured out, he'd only wound up with a headache, though, not scarred for life like those other guys.

The wounds across Eric Holt's face flashed through his mind along with the blood spattered and pooled in that alley. He wondered how the Slasher case was going back in Salt Lake, who'd taken it over and if they had found any leads.

It was easier to think about that case than about this day, about the funeral, about his dad's senseless death.

If only he'd taken better care of himself...

* * *

Kiki hated funerals because of the flood of memories they brought back. Of her parents' funeral. Of losing them both so suddenly and shockingly as she had in that traffic accident.

Fortunately, she didn't remember much about that, even though she'd been asleep in the backseat. They'd been on their way to Grandpa's for Christmas. A pang struck her heart, as it always did, when she thought of them. She still missed them so much, nearly twenty-one years later.

But Grandpa had taught her that attending funerals was the right thing to do, to pay your respects to the deceased and to offer your sympathy and support to their survivors. Robert Colton had a lot of survivors. The Colton family was big.

Ruby Colton was the one Kiki knew best because the veterinarian owned Colton Veterinary Hospital and took care of the animals for Sebastian Cross's Crosswinds Training. The two had an even closer relationship now. Sebastian's arm wrapped tightly around the blonde. He was definitely supporting her.

Ruby had three older brothers, two younger sisters and four cousins, too. A pang of envy struck Kiki. She'd always wished she had siblings. She probably had some cousins on her mother's side, but they were back in Mexico and she hadn't heard from any of them. Her grandfather had reached out, sending letters and pictures over the years, but they'd been returned as undeliverable.

Grandpa had always done his best for her. She

wrapped her arm around him, knowing that it was getting harder for him to stand for long periods of time with the arthritis he had in his back. The funeral was due to start soon, so they would be able to take a seat then.

Right now, they stood talking to Sebastian and Ruby and Ruby's mother. Jenny Colton was a strong woman. Although she was a little pale, her eyes were dry and clear. But her second oldest son must have been worried about her because he'd clearly been looking for her when he'd walked up.

Fletcher Colton. He wore a dark suit for the solemn occasion, but his hair was a little long, a little unkempt. A little sexy.

His broad shoulders strained the seams of that suit, and his eyes… They were a deep, vivid green. And his gaze was focused on her right now.

Kiki's pulse quickened at the intensity of his stare, but she tried not to take it too seriously. Fletcher Colton just seemed like an intense guy. A detective.

Detectives probably checked out everyone the way he was checking her out.

"You remember Kiki," Ruby said to him, and her lips curved into a slight smile as if she thought he had another reason for staring at her friend.

"Yes, of course," Fletcher said.

"I'm sorry for your loss," Kiki told him, repeating the words she hadn't understood when she'd been six and standing in this very room. She hadn't been able to comprehend why people were apologizing to her like they were responsible for that crash. She hadn't even known what happened for sure, since she'd been sleeping, but Grandpa had said that it was weather. No one's fault.

But now, since losing them, she had a lot more empathy. She understood how it hurt to lose a parent.

Having probably heard those words a hundred times, like she had back then, Fletcher just nodded.

"Your father did a lot for this town," her grandfather said. "He will be missed."

"Thank you, Mr. Shelton," Fletcher said. "It's great to see you."

"Don't know how long you're sticking around Owl Creek but come by if you'd like to do some fishing," Grandpa told him.

"I'm moving home," Fletcher said.

And Kiki's pulse quickened even more.

"He's taken the position of lead detective with Owl Creek Police Department," Jenny said, beaming with pride in her child.

Fletcher shrugged. "Probably won't be as busy as it was in Salt Lake City, so I'm sure I'll have time for some fishing, Mr. Shelton. Thanks for the invitation."

Since Kiki helped Grandpa with the tackle shop and fishing excursions, she would probably be seeing Fletcher around, too. That thought unsettled her for some reason.

Or maybe this uneasy feeling she had didn't have anything to do with him and it was just because he'd mentioned Salt Lake City, as it reminded her of the Slasher's recent attack outside the nightclub where Troy had been working.

Her assistant was still shaken over finding the victim, over what he'd seen. But he'd come to Owl Creek. Troy had even found a place to stay since Kiki was going to be here for the summer, helping her grandfather while doing gigs in the area. She'd booked a job at a nightclub in Conners for this upcoming weekend.

Conners was just outside Owl Creek and was just as safe. Well, just as safe since the deranged man who'd gone after Ruby had been caught.

Music began to play, signaling the beginning of the service. Mrs. Colton, Ruby and Sebastian started off toward the chairs nearest the casket. Fletcher hesitated for a moment before following them, probably dreading this.

She could totally relate.

But then he glanced at her, and there was some question in his green eyes as if he wanted to ask her something. But then he blinked, and the look was gone. He just nodded at Kiki and her grandfather, in some kind of acknowledgement, as he headed off after his family.

She and Grandpa found chairs near the back of the service, since they would have to leave right after it to check on Fancy. So Kiki probably wouldn't see Fletcher again for a while unless he actually took her grandfather up on his fishing invitation.

If he did, she'd probably make herself scarce. She had no interest in getting involved with anyone. Her career was really taking off, and when she wasn't busy working, she wanted to help Grandpa as much as she could.

She had no time for romance. No matter how good-looking Fletcher Colton was.

Not that he was interested in her. He probably just wanted to fish.

* * *

Flyers had gone up around town. Hot LA DJ Kiki Shelton was going to be spinning at Conners Club this weekend. This was an event not to be missed.

The poster had a picture of Kiki on it with her black hair, the ends dyed deep red, and her killer body. A lot of men would probably show up to watch her spin and dance.

A lot of men who would drink too much. Who would get careless.

Who might step into a dark alley.

The Slasher smiled in anticipation.

This attack was soon after the last one. The closest together of the attacks yet.

But this urge burned inside the Slasher. This urge to act again.

To lash out.

To get the attention and the revenge they deserved. And to make sure that some man in Conners got exactly what he deserved, too.

Chapter 3

As if the funeral hadn't been bad enough, Fletcher, his mom and siblings had had to meet with the estate lawyer the next day. Fortunately, he'd come out to the house and Fletcher had been able to slip out of the meeting early. Leaving the others upstairs in the great room, Fletcher slipped downstairs to the walkout level where he'd been staying in his old bedroom.

None of what the lawyer had told them had been a surprise. Jenny got the house and whatever money they'd had in their accounts. Each of the kids got an equal share of Colton Properties while Chase was named the new CEO.

It was pretty much what Fletcher would have expected, probably what they'd all expected. If they'd ever thought about their dad dying…

Even after the first stroke, Fletcher hadn't thought about it. Hadn't considered it was possible.

He'd recovered so quickly and completely from that first stroke. And even though the doctor had warned him to change his lifestyle, it hadn't really seemed possible that Robert Colton would die before he even hit sixty years old. It just hadn't seemed like it could happen.

But it did.

He was gone. But he'd been gone a lot while Fletcher and his siblings were growing up. He'd been away so much that the house didn't even feel different without him being here. Fletcher was staying with Mom, just to make sure that she wasn't alone.

Eventually he would look for his own place. But for now, it was comforting to be home, if not for Mom then at least for him. He'd already lost his dad. He didn't want anything to happen to her, too.

Kiki Shelton had lost both her parents suddenly when she'd been just a kid. When she'd said sorry at the funeral, like so many other people had, it had meant a little more because he knew she knew.

She knew even better than he did about loss.

Maybe that was why she'd intrigued him so much, why he hadn't wanted to stop talking to her even as the service started. No. That was because he'd wanted to ask her about the Slasher.

Or at least that was the idea he'd had at the time. But he realized now it was a reach. Sure. She was a DJ who worked at nightclubs. But there were a lot of nightclubs. And even if she had been at any of the ones where an attack had taken place, she would have already been questioned. She probably wouldn't have any new information to give him no matter what he'd asked her.

And that case in Salt Lake City wasn't his anymore since his dad's stroke had compelled him to cut his two-week notice short. He was glad that he'd been here, though. Glad that he'd been here for his mom and his family.

But now that the funeral was done and the will was read, it all felt so anticlimactic. So strange and surreal.

He had to get back to real life. Fortunately, he was starting at Owl Creek PD in the morning, a week earlier than he'd been scheduled to start. But he needed to get back to work. He needed to help people since he hadn't been able to help his father.

Not even the doctors had been able to help his father. Knuckles rapped against his door and then it creaked open. He turned away from the window that looked out over Blackbird Lake, surprised to see it was Chase who'd sought him out. "Everything okay?" he asked.

"I was just going to ask you that," Chase said. "You slipped out of the meeting so quickly."

"I thought it was done," Fletcher said.

Chase arched a light brown eyebrow over one of his green eyes. While he and Fletcher had the same color eyes, Chase's hair was lighter brown, and he kept it conservatively cut. And even though this meeting had been at their home, Chase wore a suit. He'd probably come right from the office, though.

Fletcher felt a pang of envy that his brother had had something to keep him busy over the past week.

"Are you upset?" Chase asked.

"About what?" Fletcher asked.

"That I was named CEO."

Fletcher chuckled and shook his head. "You were born CEO, Chase. Everybody knew that was going to happen someday."

"It happened too soon," Chase said, his voice gruff.

And Fletcher knew that even though he'd kept busy, Dad's death had probably affected his oldest brother the most. He'd certainly spent the most time with him. He closed the distance between them and pulled his brother's lean body into a brief hug. "I'm sorry..." he murmured.

And as he said the words, he thought of Kiki Shelton. Of how she'd said them.

Yeah, it was good he started his job tomorrow. Then he could get his mind off not just his dad's death but off Kiki Shelton, too. He had too much going on to even allow himself an attraction to anyone right now.

He was starting a new position with a new police department while helping his family deal with his dad's death. He didn't need any other distractions.

A couple of days had passed since the funeral, but Kiki hadn't been able to get that image of Fletcher Colton out of her mind. The way he'd looked at her...

What had he wanted to ask her?

Not that she really cared. Or had any time for it.

She needed to stop thinking about him and focus on everything else she had going on in her life. She glanced across the console of her SUV to where Fancy sat, her harness secured to the seat. The puppy whined and quivered.

"You have to get used to riding in vehicles," Kiki told her. If she went into service as a scent dog like Sebastian had predicted for her, she was going to have to travel a lot. Like Kiki did.

But a drive up toward the mountains wasn't a sacrifice at all. She loved coming out this way to Crosswinds Training Center, with the enormous sparkling blue of Blackbird Lake on one side of it and the mountains behind it.

Her heart stretched with love for this place where she'd grown up. Owl Creek was beautiful. And there was actually a creek—well, more of a river—by that name, too. It curved around and through town and emptied into the lake.

Kiki had to steer her SUV around those curves on her way up to the training center. Fancy needed a checkup, and Ruby was working out of the medical offices there today.

Kiki had been a bit surprised that she was working at all. She couldn't even remember much of that time immediately after her parents had died. Just the funeral and Grandpa.

He'd gotten a puppy then as if it would make her feel better. And somehow it had worked.

Fancy, with her tan fur and black muzzle, reminded her of that dog. Buster. Even now, years after he'd passed, Kiki remembered Buster. He'd helped her through a rough time. Just like some of the dogs that Sebastian

Cross helped train were used as PTSD dogs to help veterans, like him, through a rough time.

Maybe that was why Ruby had chosen to work, to take care of the animals she loved so much. But, remembering how closely Sebastian had stuck by Ruby's side during the funeral, it wasn't just the animals that the veterinarian loved at Crosswinds. Or that loved her.

A wistful sigh slipped out of Kiki's lips. Not that she was jealous or anything. She liked her life exactly as it was. Focused on Grandpa and growing her brand as a DJ and building her nest egg.

Fancy whined again.

"And you…" Kiki murmured. She enjoyed volunteering with these puppies as much as her grandfather did. A veteran himself, he liked helping out with the ones who were trained to assist with PTSD. But Fancy was special.

Sebastian thought so, and so did Kiki. But probably for different reasons.

"Hang in there, sweet thing," she said as she steered her SUV down the last part of the private road and onto the Crosswinds property. In addition to the big brick and wood training center, there were indoor and outdoor kennels and the medical building. "We're here," she said as she pulled up next to the medical building.

Sebastian also had a cabin on the property that he'd renovated some time ago. He had transformed it from the family getaway it had once been into his home now. Crosswinds was an ideal place with the view of the lake below and the mountains behind it, but Kiki preferred to be on the water.

When she had a gig in Owl Creek or nearby, she often went "home" to the houseboat her grandpa had on the lake instead of back to his cottage. That way she didn't risk waking him up. Maybe she would stay there tonight when she came back from the club in Conners.

She parked the SUV, then went around and opened the passenger's door. As she leaned inside to release Fancy from her seat harness, the puppy's furry body quivered with excitement, and the little dog licked Kiki's hands and then her face.

Kiki chuckled and helped the puppy down from the vehicle, holding tightly to her leash so she didn't run off. That wasn't a really big concern, though, since Fancy tended to stick close to her. "Checkup time," she said as she led the little dog toward the medical building.

Maybe Fancy understood what she'd said because she tugged against the leash, as if trying to head back toward the SUV. Maybe she remembered being here in the kennels and preferred Grandpa's cozy cottage. Kiki had been spoiling her a bit.

She'd also been working with her, though, on commands. "Heel," she said.

The puppy tensed for a moment.

"Walk."

And Fancy trotted along beside her.

"She's coming along," Sebastian said as he opened the door for her.

Kiki smiled. "She's very smart, so it doesn't take much to train her." But she still had a few bad habits, like chewing things she shouldn't. This time it had been one of Grandpa's favorite slippers.

"I really appreciate you and your grandfather helping out, though," Sebastian said. He crouched down and let the puppy sniff his hand, her little black muzzle wrinkling as she smelled the scent of other animals on him. "She's going to be good to go soon."

Kiki felt a little pang. Sure. She knew scent dogs were necessary for a variety of things, for sniffing out drugs or explosives or for tracking missing persons. But she didn't want to think of the dog ever being in harm's way because of her abilities.

Through the open door behind Sebastian, another person stepped out. Della Winslow was a couple of years older than Kiki, with long, light brown hair and brown eyes. She was a K9 search and rescue tracker, and her black lab, Charlie, was close by her side as usual.

Fancy yipped at the lab, either with excitement or fear. Kiki tugged on her leash as the puppy tried to clamor around the bigger, male dog.

"I'm sorry," Kiki said.

"Charlie is used to it," Della assured her with a smile.

"This is the pup I've been telling you about," Sebastian said. "The one out of Sable's litter."

"I remember the litter," Della said. "But you placed them with foster families so quickly, I didn't get to know any of them very well."

In addition to her job with Search and Rescue, Della also worked as a trainer at Crosswinds. She crouched down to pet the puppy, looking her over, and nodded. "I see the potential." She glanced up at Kiki. "You and your grandfather always do such a great job socializing the pups."

"You'll have to choose one to keep one of these days," Sebastian suggested.

Kiki shrugged. "I'd love to, but I travel so much. I'll mention it to my grandfather, though."

Sebastian chuckled. "He always says that he fosters them for your sake, but I think he enjoys having them, too."

Or he remembered how much Buster had comforted her and thought she still needed comforting for some reason. "He really does do a lot for my sake," Kiki said.

And she could never repay him enough for all the love and support he'd given her. So she wouldn't ask him to keep a dog for her if it really would be too much for him.

"I think it's mutual," Sebastian said. "You would do anything for him. You could still be working out in LA or Vegas, but you always come home to help him in the summer."

She shrugged again. "I enjoy playing some of the smaller venues around here."

"I saw your flyers up around town for the Conners Club tonight," Della said.

Troy had put up all the flyers. It had given him something to do, to get his mind off that attack in Salt Lake City. "Come out if you can," Kiki encouraged them.

Della gave her a noncommittal nod. But then she probably couldn't commit, never knowing what might come up that would require her help as Search and Rescue.

Sebastian grinned. "Ask Ruby—"

"Ask Ruby what?" the veterinarian asked. She stood in that open door behind Della.

Della smiled and said, "I better get going. Thanks for checking Charlie out for me. He's just been a little off lately."

Kiki could relate. She'd felt a little off since seeing Fletcher Colton at the funeral. Why did she keep thinking about him? It was good that she had a gig tonight, something else to think about besides him and how good-looking he was.

She knew there was a bachelor party that would be stopping in because the best man had messaged her some special song requests. Based on a couple of those requests, she might suggest the groom pick another best man.

"I know you were concerned that Charlie has been sleeping so much, but he's fine," Ruby assured Della. "Might just be a little bored."

That was probably Kiki's issue as well. The reason for her giving Fletcher Colton a second thought—just boredom. Once she was playing and the crowd was dancing, she would forget all about Fletcher.

Della smiled. "Well, in our business, being bored isn't a bad thing."

"It is in mine," Kiki said.

The others chuckled, and Fancy jumped up with excitement over the mood. "Down," Kiki said.

And the little dog immediately dropped down to all fours.

"Yes, she is going to be good," Della agreed with a glance at Sebastian.

Kiki wondered for a moment if they were talking about Fancy or about her. But Della rushed off and so did Sebastian, leaving Kiki alone with her friend.

"So, what was Sebastian telling you to ask me?" Ruby asked as she led the way back to an exam room.

Kiki lifted Fancy onto the table and let the nervous pup lick her face again. "About coming to the club in Conners tonight."

Ruby smiled. "I've been a little tired lately."

"After everything you've been through, that's totally understandable," Kiki said. "I'm sorry again about your dad and that whole..."

"Madman trying to kill me because he thought I was preventing him from getting this land away from Sebastian?" Ruby finished for her. "It's all over now. And it worked out." She touched her stomach and smiled again.

Kiki gasped. "Are you pregnant?"

Her smile widened, and her green eyes sparkled with happiness. "Yes."

"You and Sebastian...?"

Ruby nodded. "Yes, I've actually moved in with him."

"I'm happy for you," Kiki said, and she felt that traitorous little jab of envy again. Not that she wanted a baby or even a significant other. But sometimes, even in a crowded club, she felt so alone. That was another reason she loved to come home to Grandpa in Owl Creek. But then she shouldn't have had that feeling here.

"What about you?" Ruby asked.

Kiki patted her stomach and hips. "I'm not pregnant. Just curvy."

Ruby snorted. "You're perfect, and you know it. I meant what about your love life?"

Kiki snorted now. "What love life?"

"Exactly. How can someone like you not have a significant other?"

"I do," Kiki said.

And Ruby's eyes widened.

"My grandpa," Kiki said. "And this little nugget of cuteness here." She pressed a kiss to the top of Fancy's furry head.

Ruby chuckled. "This little nugget isn't going to stay little long. She's growing like crazy. What was your concern about her?"

"She ate part of one of Grandpa's slippers."

Ruby took out a stethoscope and listened to the puppy's belly. "How long ago was this?"

"Had to be sometime during the night. The only time Grandpa takes them off when he's in the house is when he's in bed. He didn't notice until he went to put them on this morning."

"Did she go out this morning?" Ruby asked.

Kiki nodded. "I let her out before I knew about the slipper. But I think she passed it. I just want to make sure that she's all right."

"Everything sounds fine," Ruby said. She pulled a small puppy snack from her pocket and held it out for Fancy who gobbled it up. "She has an appetite, too."

The little muzzle wrinkled as Fancy's nose sniffed the air and then Ruby's pocket. The vet chuckled and gave her another treat. "That's your reward for sniffing it out. She does have a natural talent."

"Sebastian does, too, because he already figured she'll be a scent dog," Kiki said. "He really knows what he's doing."

Ruby smiled. "Yes, he does."

"Guess I didn't have to tell you that," Kiki said with a chuckle of her own.

"Nope. We're going to be getting married soon," Ruby shared. "After what happened with us and with Dad, it just proves how short life can be and how very precious." She touched her stomach again.

Kiki laid her hand over Ruby's. "I'm so happy that something good came out of everything you've gone through recently."

Ruby blinked and smiled at her. "Of course, you'll have to be at the wedding."

"I'd love to DJ it," Kiki assured her.

"I meant as a bridesmaid," Ruby said. "I didn't expect you to work it. I'm not even sure how big a wedding we'll have. There has been so much going on here."

"Too much for you," Kiki said.

"Too much for Owl Creek," Ruby said.

"Hopefully everything will quiet down now," Kiki said.

Ruby nodded heartily in agreement but then added, "But not so much that you get bored and head back to LA early. Or that Fletcher heads back to Salt Lake City. He's used to being a lot busier than he'll be here, even with Owl Creek PD covering some of the surrounding areas."

Kiki hadn't considered that—that Fletcher might not stick around Owl Creek. She felt another strange twinge. "Do you think he'd leave?"

"Not anytime soon," Ruby said. "He's worried about Mom. We all are. But she's doing really well."

"That's good."

"Good that Mom's doing well or that Fletcher will be staying?"

Heat rushed to Kiki's face. "I don't even know Fletcher." She sighed. "Don't be one of those happy brides-to-be that tries matching up all their friends now."

Ruby held up her hands. "I promise I won't. I'm really busy. It was just the way you two looked at each other at the funeral…"

Fletcher wasn't the only one in his family who'd been intensely studying her then. Ruby must have been, too. But Kiki had only noticed Fletcher. Despite the warmth of the June day, a little shiver raced down her spine.

"Your pregnancy must be causing hallucinations," Kiki teased. "I doubt Fletcher is any more interested in me than I am in him. And now I better get this little fur ball back to Grandpa and start loading up my equipment for my gig tonight. Sure you won't come?"

Ruby yawned. "Maybe another time."

Kiki nodded. "Sure. Take care."

"You, too."

And Kiki felt that little shiver again. She was safe. Wasn't she? It wasn't as if anything would happen at the Conners Club that had happened at those other clubs.

Those had been in bigger cities, more dangerous areas of town.

Conners wasn't much bigger than Owl Creek, so hopefully it was just as safe as Kiki had assured Troy that it was. Nothing bad was going to happen here.

This music was so much better than what had played in Salt Lake City. It was more alive, more melodious, and made the Slasher feel as if it had been mixed to choreograph to their movements, to the swing and swish of the blade cutting through the air and then cutting through the next victim.

He screamed and lifted his hands to his bleeding face. And the Slasher cut through those as well.

And when the hands fell away and the victim dropped to the asphalt in the alley, the Slasher slashed some more...

Chapter 4

His first few days on the job had been uneventful. Despite being lead detective, Fletcher hadn't had many investigations to lead. A stolen vehicle. A suspected driving under the influence incident. The most exciting thing had been a possible embezzlement of a school's booster fund by one of the parents.

With as close as the police department was to his sister Frannie's bookstore café, Book Mark It, at least he'd been able to stop in and visit her a few times. Check on her. They'd always been super close growing up. Not that he had liked books the way she had, but they'd both loved a good mystery.

After some of the things he'd seen in Salt Lake City, like the latest victim of the Slasher, Fletcher should have been relieved that, despite what had happened with

Ruby and Sebastian, his hometown was relatively safe and quiet. He *was* relieved for the sake of his family.

But for himself...

Fletcher loved working. Maybe he'd gotten that from his dad. But unlike his dad, Fletcher knew that his overwhelming love of his job meant he was better off single than trying to have a wife and family. He didn't want to miss all the things that his father had over the years. But not working wasn't an option for him.

He had to work. Had cases to solve, criminals to catch and put away even in Owl Creek. So he'd focused on the car thief, the drunk driver and the embezzler and had closed those cases. At least Owl Creek PD covered Conners as well, but nothing had come up yet there that they hadn't been able to handle on their own.

Until Fletcher's phone rang in the early morning hours of Saturday. His cell vibrated across the surface of the bedside table and he reached out for it, answering with a groggy, "Colton."

"Fletcher?"

It was the chief, his boss, so Fletcher roused himself. "Yes, sir."

"You've been requested to help out with an assault that just happened in Conners."

"Requested? Me specifically?" he asked. How did anyone in Conners even know he'd accepted the job at Owl Creek PD?

"You're needed at the crime scene there," the chief continued.

"Needed? Requested? I'm confused, Chief," he admitted.

"Conners PD know there've been some cases like this in Salt Lake City when you were there," the chief explained. "So they need you out at the crime scene ASAP."

Fletcher went from groggy with sleep to wide-awake and tense. "Cases like what?"

"Where a guy is found in an alley behind a club and he's been viciously attacked—"

"The Slasher."

Here? In the Owl Creek area?

Not the big clubs in the big cities.

It didn't make sense, but that made it even more interesting. "Is the guy all right?" He asked the most important question.

Had the attacks escalated, like he'd been worrying they were? Had it become more than assault?

"He's alive," the chief said. "I don't know any more about his condition or what happened. Just that they'd like you to advise." And he gave him the address of the crime scene.

"I'll be there." Fletcher rolled out of bed and dressed in a rush, desperate to get to the nightclub in Conners before it was too late, before all the witnesses were gone. But as fast as he'd dressed and drove, he still arrived too late to interview the victim. And most of the guests had left the club.

Fletcher got an almost dizzying sense of déjà vu. The location was so similar to the last crime scene where he turned up in the alley as the techs were processing it. The blood pools and spatters were the same. "Let me guess," he said. "No footprints? No evidence?"

One of the techs looked up at him, her eyes narrowed with suspicion. "We're not giving interviews."

"That's good," Fletcher said. "Because I think the Slasher is getting off on the notoriety."

Why else had the perp stepped up his attacks? If their victims were really random, then the only reason would have been for more attention. For more media coverage.

The reporters had been out front, but Fletcher had slipped through them unnoticed and then flashed his badge at the officer guarding the entrance to the alley. He flashed it now at the tech. "I'm the lead detective with Owl Creek PD."

The young woman nodded. "I heard they were sending somebody over since we're short-staffed. Right now, we're processing everything. Hopefully we find something."

"If you don't, you won't be the only techs who couldn't," he assured her.

"You've worked these cases before?"

"Not like I've wanted to," he admitted. The first one he hadn't been assigned as he'd had other cases to close first. And the second…

His dad had had the stroke, and Fletcher had been called home early to Owl Creek. And he'd thought then that he wouldn't have the chance to work the Slasher case again.

But the Slasher had come here, too. Maybe.

"Are you sure this case matches the profile of the other ones?" he asked the tech. He couldn't imagine that, if the Slasher wanted publicity, they would choose here for their next attack. Wouldn't they go back to LA or Vegas where there was more of a media presence?

"The victim was slashed up bad across his face, hands and chest," a man said as he stepped out through the back door that was open to the interior of the club. He extended his hand toward Fletcher. "You must be Detective Colton. I'm Sergeant Powers." The man had thin gray hair and a lot of lines in his face.

Fletcher shook his hand and nodded. "I appreciate you calling me in on this."

"I appreciate you pitching in. This kind of a case is above my pay grade, especially since I'm semiretired." He yawned. "I have another officer conducting interviews with the last of the people who actually stayed in the club and didn't take off the minute the police were called."

"Sounds like that wasn't many," Fletcher remarked. That had appeared to be the same situation in Salt Lake City, too. Nobody wanted to get involved, or maybe they were worried about public intoxication or some other charge, depending on what they'd been doing in the club.

"Wrapping up now," the sergeant remarked, and he stepped away from the door so that Fletcher could see inside the club. The lights had been turned up, the harsh fluorescent bulbs illuminating the nearly empty space.

And he saw her.

She wore black, like she had when she'd attended his dad's funeral, but it wasn't a dress. She wore tight leather pants and a cropped top. And her voice was even huskier than it had sounded in the funeral parlor as she replied to the officer's question. "There's really nothing I can tell you about what happened in the alley. I was behind the turntables the whole night, usually with my headphones on."

"So you didn't see or hear anything. You can go," the uniformed officer that the sergeant had assigned to take statements told her.

While they'd called in Fletcher to help, they weren't letting him do very damn much. He'd wanted to conduct the interviews. But he wanted more than that.

He had an idea. With Kiki's help, he might have a way that he could work the case. Maybe he would actually be able to solve it and catch the Slasher.

But when he started toward the door, the sergeant stepped in front of him. "I need to pick your brain about these cases," the older man said. "See if you have any idea where we should start."

He had a damn good idea.

With Kiki Shelton.

She hadn't been lying to the officer when she'd answered his questions just moments ago. Kiki hadn't heard or seen anything. She'd had her headphones on, as she always did, while mixing the tracks. Hell, she'd even had her eyes closed, moving to the music. Feeling her own vibe.

And during that time, someone had been getting attacked in the alley.

She shuddered in horror. The same horror Troy must

have been feeling, because he'd disappeared sometime during the night, too.

She wasn't even sure when. One minute he'd been there and finally, when she'd noticed the commotion in the club, she'd also noticed he was gone.

Had he found this victim, too?

She'd thought it was one of the bachelor party guys who had discovered the injured man because he'd been waving his arms around, his hands smeared with blood.

And she'd taken off her headphones to hear him screaming for help and to hear other clubgoers yelling when they saw the blood on the man.

Everything had descended into chaos after that, with people running and shouting. And Kiki had pretty much been trapped behind the turntables, unable to get out and even look for Troy. She'd expected he would show up.

But he hadn't.

Even after the police cleared the club of whoever had actually remained behind to talk to them. While she had stayed as well, she hadn't been any help to the police. And now she had no help herself.

"Troy, where are you?" she whispered into the darkness of the back parking lot. Her SUV was out here, one of the shadows in the night. She would have clicked the fob to turn on the lights, but her hands were wrapped around the handles at the top of the speakers she rolled across the asphalt.

In addition to her turntables and mixers, Kiki always used her own sound system. Sometimes she patched it in with the club's system, but most of the time hers was better. Because she preferred her own setup, she had a lot of things to schlep from club to club.

That was why she needed an assistant. Even though she was strong enough to carry the equipment on her own, if she was working alone, she had to take more trips for set-up and breakdown. And breakdown, at the end of a long night, needed to be faster because by that time all she wanted to do was go home, shower and drop into her bed and sleep.

That probably wouldn't be possible tonight, not when she was worrying about that poor man. There had been all that blood just on his friend.

How much had there been on the victim?

She didn't want to think about it, but her maudlin mind kept circling back there, to the alley where he'd been found. She'd done her best to keep to the other direction, which was thankfully where she'd parked.

Before the attack, the club owner had offered to let her and Troy unload and load up their equipment in that alley, but Troy had shuddered and refused, saying that he never wanted to set foot in another one after the last.

She'd promised him then that nothing like that would happen around Owl Creek. She'd promised him it was safe here. That the Slasher wouldn't attack anyone here.

Had it been the Slasher?

Maybe it had just been some random mugging.

Not that it made anyone any safer.

In fact, it probably made them less safe because then there were, potentially, two dangerous people out there: a mugger and the Slasher.

No. Not here. Not this close to home.

She shivered despite the warmth of the June evening and hastened her pace across the parking lot. But footsteps echoed hers. She glanced over her shoulder, but nothing was visible in the dark but darker shadows.

What had happened to the streetlights out here? Were there any? It had been light when she and Troy had parked out here, his truck next to her SUV.

She turned back to where they'd parked, but it looked like only one vehicle was still out there. Hers.

Troy had left.

So who was behind her?

She heard the footsteps again, the scrape of shoe soles against the asphalt. Her pulse quickening with fear, she released the handle on the speaker and reached inside the bag slung over her shoulder. She wasn't looking for the key fob. She was looking for her pepper spray.

Nobody was getting close enough to slash her.

Chapter 5

Where the hell was she?

He could hear something in the darkness, something like wheels rolling over asphalt. Like someone was moving a suitcase or something...

Curious, he'd followed the noise. But in the darkness, he couldn't see anything. He'd considered turning on his light and calling out. But what if it was the Slasher?

He uttered a short, derisive snort at the thought. The Slasher hadn't avoided getting caught all this time by hanging around the crime scenes. They probably moved on to the next city shortly after an attack.

But why here?

"Don't try anything! I have pepper spray!" a voice called from the darkness.

"Kiki, it's me," Fletcher said as he turned on the flashlight on his phone. The beam illuminated her standing in the middle of the dark parking lot, a small canister clutched in her hand, her finger ready to press the sprayer.

"It's Fletcher," he clarified. Since he was still in the dark, she probably couldn't see him. So he moved the light closer to his face.

"What the hell…" She released a shaky breath. "Why didn't you say anything? You scared me!"

"I'm sorry," he said. "I couldn't see who was out here either."

"What are you even doing here?" she asked. "You weren't in the club tonight."

Maybe it hadn't been that busy then, since she sounded so certain that she hadn't seen him there. Or maybe she just assumed, correctly, that he wasn't the type to go to clubs. They were too loud. Too crowded. Too full of drunk, obnoxious partiers that he dealt with all too often already as a detective.

"After the person was found in the alley, the Conners Police Department called us in to assist."

She released another shaky breath. "Oh, that makes sense."

Apparently, more sense to her than him being at the club having a good time.

But she wasn't wrong. Fletcher couldn't actually remember the last time he'd had a good time. Certainly not since his dad's stroke and…

"Did you think it was the attacker out here?" she asked and shuddered.

"I didn't know what to think," he said and pointed

to the canister in her hand. "Evidently neither did you." But he was glad that she'd been prepared to defend herself had it been necessary.

"This is so damn scary," she said. "People getting attacked like that so viciously." She shuddered again.

"You were prepared with the pepper spray," he said. "But you really shouldn't be out here alone in the dark like this. It's too dangerous. And I'm not just talking about the Slasher. Anyone from the club could have followed you out here."

Her lips curved into a faint smile. "You're the only 'anyone' out here besides me. And you sound like my grandfather."

"Jim Shelton is a very wise man," Fletcher said.

"He worries too much. And after this…" She sighed. "He's going to worry even more."

Fletcher had an idea.

A solution to her problem and maybe to his as well. "Maybe we can figure out a way to allay his fears," he said.

"We? What are you talking about?" she asked.

He glanced around that all-enveloping blankness. Anybody could be out there, hiding in the dark. Even the Slasher.

"Let's talk about it somewhere else," he said. "What are you doing out here?"

She thumped her hand against the top of what looked like a speaker on wheels. "Putting my equipment in my vehicle."

"You parked way out here?" he asked.

She sighed. "It didn't seem that way out when it was still daylight."

"And you're moving all this equipment on your own?"

"I have an assistant."

Fletcher swung the beam of his cell flashlight around the area. But he only saw the two of them. "Where is your *assistant*?"

She sighed again, and this one was heavy. "I don't know. I haven't seen him since the lights came up and the police were called."

"He just took off?"

"A lot of people did," she said. "It was chaos."

"Why?" he asked.

"A man was attacked," she said. "People were screaming. There was blood." She shuddered now, more violently than she had before.

"You saw the victim?"

She shook her head. "No. The guy who found him, his friend, had blood on his hands and shirt and he was screaming for help." Her voice cracked with emotion, with empathy.

"So instead of helping him, people took off," Fletcher pointed out. "Including your assistant, leaving you to move all your equipment on your own."

"I'm sure he was just shaken up like everyone else," Kiki said. "They didn't know how to react. They were just scared, especially Troy. I assured him it would be safe here after Salt Lake City."

"What do you mean?" Fletcher asked. "Just because of what happened there with the Slasher? Or were you there?"

"I wasn't," Kiki said. "But Troy was. He found that victim, and it really freaked him out. I promised him that it was safer here, that nothing would happen."

This Troy had been at the scene of two of the attacks.

Fletcher needed to find her assistant. "When did you last see Troy?"

She shrugged. "I don't know. I was so busy with special requests and people coming up. I don't remember when I saw him last."

So he could have slipped into the alley before the attack.

"Did you try calling him?" Fletcher asked. "Texting him?"

"Yeah, of course," she replied. "But I didn't get any reply or even his voice mail. It's like his phone is dead or off or something."

Fletcher suspected the *or something*. Like the man took his cell apart so that nobody could track him. And Fletcher could think of one reason why.

So no one would find out he was the Slasher.

Instead of a police escort, Kiki had had just one lawman tailing her home. Why?

She doubted he was concerned about her safety; she didn't fit the profile of the Slasher's usual victims. She wasn't male. And she was pretty sure, from the way he looked at her, that Fletcher Colton was well aware of that. Just as she was well aware of how very male he was.

Her pulse quickened, but that had to be because of what had happened that night.

She hadn't seen the victim, but she'd seen all that blood on his friend. That poor man.

Who would do such a thing to someone? Attack them so viciously?

Kiki turned her SUV into the driveway of her grandfather's cottage. Lights shone in her back window as a vehicle pulled in behind hers. Fletcher's. He got out of his SUV at the same time she stepped out of hers. "You didn't need to follow me home," she told him.

"You have all that stuff to unload," he said, waving his hand at the rear hatch of her SUV.

He'd helped her load up the rest of her equipment at the nightclub.

"I leave it in there," she said. "There really isn't any room for it in the cottage." Her grandfather's house was small, so she had more storage space in the back of her SUV. With the tinted windows, it was hard to see the expensive equipment stored inside so she didn't worry about it getting stolen.

She hadn't thought she needed to worry about those Slasher attacks here in Owl Creek either, though. Maybe she needed to be more careful. "I should grab my laptop, though," she said, clicking open the hatch.

As it rose, the front door of the house opened and the yard light flashed on, illuminating the driveway while leaving the man standing in the doorway in the shadows.

Jim called out, "You okay?"

She sucked in a breath, worried that he might have heard about the attack already. "I'm fine, Grandpa."

Fancy pushed past him in the doorway and ran out to the SUV, bouncing around Kiki's and Fletcher's legs.

"I heard a man's voice," Grandpa said, "and I wanted to make sure you were all right."

"Fletcher Colton is out here with me," she said, though her grandfather could probably see that for himself now.

"I was just making sure she got home safely, sir," Fletcher called back to Grandpa.

"Something happen?" the older man asked.

Kiki smothered the groan trying to slip out of her throat. Before Fletcher could say anything about the attack, which would upset her grandfather and keep him awake, she grabbed his hand, squeezing it to shut him up and also to make her grandfather think that they were together. "No. He was just being a gentleman, Grandpa."

"Few of them left nowadays," Grandpa said. "I'll leave you two alone then." He chuckled. "Well, except for that little furry chaperone."

Fancy still hopped around on the driveway but her interest appeared to be more in the back of the SUV than in them, since her little muzzle wrinkled as she sniffed. She was so focused that she didn't even react when the door closed behind Grandpa.

"What's she smelling?" Fletcher asked, and his long body seemed to tense next to Kiki, reminding her that she was holding his hand.

She jerked hers away, her skin tingling in reaction. "I don't know. Sebastian thinks she'll be a scent dog. I think he's right."

"Drugs?"

She tensed now with righteous indignation. "What are you saying? You think I have drugs in my vehicle?"

Fletcher held up his hands. "I was just asking what he was training the dog to sniff out."

"Nothing yet," Kiki replied. "Fancy has to get socialized first and learn basic commands. Like Sit." And she turned toward the puppy, held her hand out—palm up—at waist level and then raised it toward her shoulder.

Fancy whined and danced around for a moment.

"Sit." She repeated the gesture and finally Fancy planted her little squirmy butt on the ground. The dog was smart. They'd only been working together a couple of weeks, and she was already beginning to master the basic commands. Kiki reached into the back of the SUV and pulled out her laptop bag. In the front pocket was a small packet of puppy treats. She rewarded Fancy with one. "That's what she was sniffing out. Her treats. Not drugs."

"You're a little defensive."

"I hate that people assume, just because I work in nightclubs, that I'm either a user or a dealer." She groaned her disgust at that all too common assumption. "There are a lot of people who go to nightclubs to listen to music and dance and just have a good time."

"That guy tonight—in the alley—he didn't have a good time," Fletcher said. "The other victims of the Slasher, disfigured for life, didn't have a good time."

She flinched. "I know. But that had nothing to do with the music or the nightclub."

"Those attacks have only happened outside night-clubs," Fletcher said. "So they definitely have something to do with nightclubs. So does your assistant."

She sucked in a breath. "You suspect Troy?"

"You don't?"

A laugh bubbled out of her, but it cracked a bit with nerves. "God, no. I can't believe you do. He was devastated when he found that body in Salt Lake City. And tonight."

"Yes, what happened to him tonight?" Fletcher asked. "Where did he go?"

She shrugged. "I don't know. I'm sure he just got freaked out that it happened here after I promised him it was safer in Owl Creek. I told him things like that didn't happen here."

"Things like that can happen anywhere," Fletcher said.

As a detective, he probably could have given her examples, but he didn't need to. She knew what had nearly happened to his sister Ruby here.

She just sighed. "I know. And I shouldn't have made him a promise I couldn't keep. He's probably angry and disillusioned—"

"Or guilty," Fletcher interjected. "I need to talk to him. Tell me where he is."

She shivered at his tone and his intensity. Now she knew why Fletcher had been hired as lead detective. He could probably get a confession out of anyone with that look, that edge to his voice.

Probably even out of an innocent person, which was

what she believed Troy was. But Troy was also a bit flighty at times, emotional, reactive.

That had to be why he'd taken off like he had. He was scared. And Fletcher interrogating him would scare him even more.

"I've known Troy for four or five years now," she said. "He's a good guy. He works hard and is very helpful."

"Helpful to whom?" Fletcher asked with a pointed glance into the back of her SUV.

"He would have helped me with this equipment, but that attack, so soon after the last one, must have scared him," she said, her voice heavy with concern for her friend and for the victim. "That's why he took off like he did."

"Without a word to you," Fletcher said. "Without checking to make sure you were okay."

"I'm okay," Kiki said. "I was in the club the whole time. I was never in danger."

Fletcher nodded. "No, you weren't. You're not the Slasher's usual victim." His gaze flicked down her body in her leather pants and cropped top. "You're definitely not male."

And despite the warmth of the June night, Kiki shivered a little with goosebumps, not of cold but of awareness, rising on her skin. "Are you flirting with me, Detective?" she asked.

His lips curved into a slight grin. "Just making an observation."

She smiled and mused, "Strange observation to be making during the course of your investigation." Then, because she'd been wondering, she asked, "Why did you follow me home?"

Fletcher chuckled and his grin widened. "You definitely aren't in any danger," he said. "You're too perceptive to have anyone sneak up on you."

"Are you trying to sneak up on me?" she asked. "Just as I was never in any danger, I wasn't the danger either, in case you consider me a suspect. I was behind the turntables in front of a hell of a lot of witnesses when that attack must have taken place. And I was here when the man in Salt Lake City was attacked."

She'd been in some of the same cities for those other attacks, but she wasn't about to point that out to him. Not when he clearly considered her assistant a suspect.

"Troy was there," he said, confirming his suspicion. "And I need you to help me find him so I can question him. Will you do that?"

She sighed and nodded. "Only because I know that once you question him, he'll be able to provide alibis and prove his innocence to you."

"Let's hope that's the case," he said.

"Liar," she said. "You'd probably like it to be Troy, so that you can close this case."

"You are perceptive," he said. "The Slasher needs to be stopped. What he's doing to these victims is so cruel, and eventually one of them will probably die from their injuries."

She shivered again with revulsion and dread. "You're right. I'll help you find Troy. But what happens when you realize he's not the Slasher? How will you catch this person then?"

He looked at her again, his forehead furrowing beneath the strands of his overly long hair. And that intensity was back in his green eyes.

The intensity that unsettled her for a lot of reasons.

"I have an idea about how I can do that," he said.

"Why do I feel like that idea involves me?" she asked uneasily.

His grin widened even more, and his green eyes glinted in the light from the porch. "Because you are perceptive."

His idea definitely involved her.

Chapter 6

Fletcher was certain that Kiki wasn't in danger from the Slasher, which was the only reason he'd considered the idea he'd had to be able to investigate from the inside of the nightclub scene. But before he shared that plan with her, he wanted to find out if it was even necessary or if the first real suspect in the case was the Slasher.

Her assistant. Troy.

"You really don't know his last name?" he asked with suspicion as he glanced across the console to the passenger's seat of his SUV. Fancy rode in the back, her harness strapped to the seat.

"No, I don't," she said, her voice a little sharp with either irritation or maybe embarrassment.

"You said you've known him for four or five years."

"I have."

"And he's your assistant. Don't you have to have his full name to put on his paycheck?"

"He just takes a share of the tips. He doesn't want a paycheck."

"He doesn't want to pay taxes," Fletcher concluded.

"You have to pay taxes on tips." Kiki said it so matter-of-factly that it was clear she would never consider not declaring them.

He doubted that Troy was as conscientious about that as she was. The man was either avoiding income taxes or child support or maybe both. What else was he running from? Fletcher doubted that it was really the Slasher.

Every one of the victims had been a clubgoer, not someone who worked at the club. But someone like this Troy, who went from club to club... He made a very interesting suspect.

By that line of thinking, so did Kiki. He would have to double-check her story that she had been working the entire evening. That she hadn't taken a break at all.

And he had an idea of how he could check her story.

If it was necessary.

But if this mysterious Troy was really the Slasher, then Fletcher had no reason to spend any more time with Kiki Shelton. A pang of disappointment struck him at the thought.

But that was ridiculous, just as flirting with Kiki had been silly. She was Ruby's friend, and Ruby had already been through too much even before they'd lost their dad. The last thing his sister needed right now was Fletcher creating any awkwardness with her friend, who was also someone who fostered dogs for Ruby's soon-to-be husband Sebastian.

And Fletcher was pretty certain it would end in awkwardness, as most of his relationships had. Either he got ghosted—like his girlfriends believed he was ghosting them when he was simply busy—or he got cheated on because someone else gave them more time and attention than he was able to.

No. He had no business flirting with Kiki Shelton. But he couldn't stop glancing across the console at her. She was so beautiful, and the way the black leather clung to the curves of her body had his body tensing with desire for her. He had to ignore his attraction to her, though, and focus on the case.

The Slasher could not claim any more victims.

He slowed his SUV and turned into the driveway for the seasonal RV park where Kiki said that her assistant had parked his van. He drove past some high-end travel trailers and motor homes toward the outskirts of the RV park where the woods had begun to claim back the cleared areas. In a section of weeds, someone had parked a vintage VW bus.

"That's it," Kiki said. "He's here!"

The van was dark, like the other vehicles parked around it. "How do you know?" he asked.

"He drove that to the club tonight," she said. "It wouldn't be here unless he'd driven it back."

So he was here. This close.

The Slasher?

Fletcher reached for his weapon as Kiki reached for

the door handle. "No," he told her. "You need to stay here. Wait until I make sure he isn't a threat."

"He isn't," Kiki insisted. "Not to me."

"But if he considers you being here a threat, he's going to be one, too. Somebody dangerous is hazardous to anyone who gets in their way," Fletcher said.

In denial or defense of her friend, she shook her head. But she didn't open the door.

Fletcher stepped out into the darkness and listened. Gravel crunched. Twigs snapped and there was a subtle shift in the air, indicating movement around him. It could have been other RV residents or animals. But somehow, he suspected it wasn't.

He drew his weapon and his flashlight and aimed his beam around the area as he approached the van. Tree limbs rustled. Something was definitely out there.

Or someone.

"Police," Fletcher called out, identifying himself even though he really didn't want to, just in case he needed to fall back on his other plan. The one he had yet to bring up to Kiki.

But whoever, or whatever, was out there didn't come out of the trees. More branches rustled but the sounds were farther away now and getting fainter as the person fled. So when Fletcher shined his light into the van, he wasn't surprised to find it empty.

Troy had taken off again.

The passenger's door opened, and Kiki stepped out. "He's gone?"

"Yes."

Fletcher touched the handle of one of the back doors

of the van, and it easily opened. Troy had run off in such a hurry that he'd left it unlocked.

Another door opened and then Fancy rushed up next to Fletcher. The van was lower to the ground, so the puppy easily jumped inside, sniffing through the bedding and belongings tossed about the back of the van.

Then she yipped and pulled something from the bedding and brought it toward Fletcher. He shone his light through the clear plastic to the collection of different colored capsules inside it. The puppy's sharp teeth were already tearing through the bag.

And Kiki gasped with concern. Then she pointed toward the ground. "Drop!"

Fancy whined.

"Drop!"

And the little teeth released the bag, dropping it onto the threadbare carpet next to Fletcher. "Some little pharmacy he has here," he mused.

"These could be his," Kiki said, but even she sounded doubtful now. But she scooped Fancy up in her arms and lifted her out of the back of the van.

"Troy has a medical condition?" he asked.

She sighed. "Not that I know of."

He shone his light over the van, watching for it to glint off metal. And it did. Off beer cans. Not a knife blade.

She tensed and turned toward him. "Don't you have to have a warrant or something to search his premises?"

"Nobody has seen him since the attack," he said. "I have probable cause to make sure that he's all right."

"You can't take those pills," she said. "What if they are medically necessary?"

Fletcher snorted in derision at that, but he didn't have a warrant, as she'd pointed out. He really shouldn't have even opened the door to the van.

And he had no right to open the glove box either. So he shut the door. Then he made a note of the license plate number. He'd run that, see if he could find out Troy's last name and if the van was actually registered to him.

Instead of releasing the puppy, Kiki snuggled it against her as if she needed comforting.

"You're not so sure of your assistant's innocence anymore," Fletcher remarked.

"I know he's not the Slasher," she insisted. "But the drugs…" She sighed again. "Sometimes he seems a little out of it. I thought maybe he drank too much."

"There were a lot of beer cans in the van," Fletcher said.

"And that bag of all those drugs."

"So maybe some of those people who approach you for drugs do it not because of your working in a night-club but because of Troy?" he asked.

A little breath of air hissed through her teeth. "I don't want to think that."

But she clearly was thinking it now.

"So from his disappearing act, it looks like you're going to need a new assistant," he said.

"I'll be able to find someone here in Owl Creek," she replied. "I know a lot of people willing to help me out."

"You don't have to look any further," Fletcher told her.

"What do you mean?"

But instead of answering her, he just opened the back door of his vehicle for her to buckle Fancy back inside. Then he opened her door too before heading around the hood to his side. He glanced around him again, feeling someone out there. Watching them.

Listening to them.

So he wasn't going to ask her here.

Kiki knew that Fletcher had a plan that somehow involved her. But he didn't share it with her that night. Or that early morning.

He just dropped her and Fancy back at Jim's and drove away, leaving her wondering. Awake. And worried.

He must not have slept either because he returned a few hours later, pulling his SUV into the driveway behind hers. Fortunately, Jim had already left to take out a fishing charter on the lake. He had a boat docked near where the houseboat was. After last night, waking her grandfather up when Fletcher had followed her home, she probably needed to stay out on the boat, at least on the nights that she DJ'd.

Fancy barked and jumped on the door, trying to get outside to greet Fletcher before he even got out of his vehicle. "Someone's smitten…" Kiki murmured as she got up from the table where steam rose from her mug of coffee. Then, through the screen door, she watched Fletcher walking toward the house. The wind ruffled his overly long dark brown hair and plastered his shirt against his broad shoulders and muscular chest. She didn't have to be a detective to conclude that this detective worked out and that Fancy might not be the only smitten one.

But when he got up to the house and the wind was no longer blowing his clothes against his body, she could tell that they were a little oversize and wrinkly, like Grandpa's favorite TV detective that he watched reruns of nearly every day no matter how many times he'd already "solved" the case.

She pushed open the screen door and let Fancy out to bounce around his legs, pawing at his khaki pants.

He leaned down and scratched behind the puppy's ears, and the shameless mutt dropped and rolled onto her back, giving him her belly to rub. He chuckled as he scratched that fur, too. "She's seriously cute," he said, and he glanced up at Kiki, his green eyes warm with affection for the pet.

He was seriously cute, too.

She'd thought so every time their paths had crossed in the past. But with him working in Salt Lake City and her working in so many other cities, they hadn't seen each other often over the years. Not even when she came home for the summers to help Grandpa.

Because Fletcher hadn't lived in Owl Creek for a while.

"What are you doing back here?" she asked him, the curiosity overwhelming her.

He tensed for a moment. "I have an idea about how I might be able to catch the Slasher."

She shook her head.

"You're not going to hear me out?"

"No, I meant why did you come back to Owl Creek?"

she asked. "It had nothing to do with the Slasher because you probably didn't think the Slasher would show up here any more than I did."

"I came home when Ruby was in danger, and I liked how Owl Creek PD handled the case."

And they'd liked him enough to offer him the job of lead detective. "I know that. But why did you really want to come back? You could have stayed in Salt Lake City or gone somewhere else where there would be more crimes to solve."

"There are crimes here to solve," he said.

She sighed. "Not usually. I can't believe that was the Slasher last night."

"You don't want to believe it," Fletcher said. "But the MO and the wound patterns match the other victims. It was definitely the Slasher."

She sighed again, but it was ragged. And her chest ached. "You still didn't answer my question, you know."

He flashed her a grin. "Maybe you should be the detective. You're good at this interrogation thing."

She laughed. "It's one question. I'm not interrogating you. I'm..."

"What?" he asked. "Interested?"

"Curious," she corrected him. Interested implied something more like attraction, like desire...

And she actually felt those, too, but she didn't want him to know that. He and his family had already been through too much lately. And she...

She had too much going on for a serious relationship. And to her, the Coltons were serious people. At least Fletcher seemed to be with that intensity of his in the strained cord in his neck, in the twitch above his square jaw and in that stare he fixed on her.

"So, are you going to satisfy my curiosity?" she asked.

"If you'll satisfy mine sometime," he said, negotiating with her.

She smiled and shrugged. "Sure." She wasn't sure what he would ask her, but she had nothing to hide. "So…"

He shrugged now, those broad shoulders pulling the wrinkles from his oversize cotton button-down shirt. "I was worried about Ruby and noticing how much older my parents were getting. And Hannah is raising Lucy all alone." He shrugged again. "I felt like I needed to come home. I just wish I'd realized that sooner, before my dad had another stroke."

She reached out for him then, grabbing his hand to squeeze in hers. "I'm sorry."

"You offered your condolences at the funeral," he reminded her.

"But it doesn't hurt just that one day."

He turned his hand in hers and squeezed back. "You would know. I'm sorry about your parents."

She shrugged off his sympathy. "That was a long time ago."

"It doesn't hurt just that one day," he said.

She smiled at him repeating her words back to her. "So it's your turn," she said. "You can satisfy your curiosity now."

His gaze slipped then, to her lips, and his thumb rubbed across the back of her knuckles.

Saliva filled her mouth, and she had to swallow hard

so she didn't start drooling over the man. He wasn't thinking about kissing her. That wasn't the curiosity he wanted to satisfy. She was sure of that.

But then she remembered how he'd looked at her in her black leather outfit, his gaze sliding up and down her body like a caress. She wasn't wearing leather now. She was wearing very old and ragged jeans with a light cotton T-shirt. But the material was soft enough that it did cling to her curves, and the holes in the jeans revealed her tan thighs and knees.

His gaze dipped down over her again like it had the night before, and his green eyes darkened, the pupils dilating. Maybe he did want to kiss her.

She wouldn't protest. She was curious about his mouth, too. But then she reminded herself how bad an idea it was to get involved with anyone right now, least of all a Colton. He was mourning. She smiled again and stepped back, breaking the contact of their hands.

And she was busy. She had to help Grandpa with the fishing business and Fancy and...

"I need your help," Fletcher said.

"With what?" she asked slowly, reluctantly, because she'd already suspected he'd wanted to ask her to do something, something she probably wasn't going to want to do. Like when he'd asked her to show him where Troy lived.

"Did you find Troy?" she asked. Maybe he wanted her to talk to her assistant and encourage him to answer Fletcher's questions.

He shook his head. "Not yet."

"He couldn't have gotten far," she pointed out, "without his vehicle."

"I know. I have someone watching it. An APB out for him to be picked up for questioning. Hoover. That's his last name. He's Troy Hoover."

She shrugged. "I didn't know. Like I told you, it never came up."

"You didn't know his last name. Or that he's had a previous arrest for drug possession and that he owes back child support? That didn't come up either?" he asked, and he was definitely doing the interrogating now.

She shook her head. "He helped another DJ I knew, and when that DJ retired, Troy just started helping me out. It wasn't like I had him fill out a job application and checked his references."

"Or even got his last name."

"I knew him for a while—through the other DJ, through the clubs." She sighed. "But yes, I should have asked him more about himself." She couldn't deny that now, especially since he apparently had a record. "When were those arrests?"

"The drug possession was a while ago," Fletcher admitted. "And the child support is just outstanding. No arrest warrant for that yet."

"I didn't even know he had a child," she murmured.

"Two."

Two kids that he wasn't helping to support. She cursed. "I shouldn't have let him take his wages from the tips."

Fletcher shook his head. "No. That helped him evade garnishment of his wages and taxes."

She released a ragged sigh. "Well, I still don't believe he's the Slasher. But I won't let him work with me ever again either." Guilt pulled at her that she, however inadvertently, had helped him avoid his responsibilities. "I really thought I knew him better than that."

"Some people are hard to get to know," Fletcher said.

And she suspected he was one of them. Although he had eventually answered her question about his return, he had yet to tell her what his plan was and how it involved her.

"Yes, they are," she agreed with a pointed look.

He chuckled. "I'm an open book."

"So read the chapter heading to me about why you're here then," she urged him.

"You need an assistant," he said.

She narrowed her eyes and studied his face. "I have managed on my own." But it was work.

"You don't need to. I know someone you can use as your assistant," he said.

"Really? Who is that?"

"Me."

She closed her eyes and tried to picture him—in his wrinkly business casual khakis and button-down cotton shirt, standing behind the turntables with her—and a laugh bubbled out of her at the image. "Everybody would know you're a cop."

He shook his head. "No. I just started the job, and I didn't interview anyone in Conners last night. Only a tech and the sergeant saw me. And I haven't been around much since I moved away from Owl Creek, so most people won't recognize me."

"People might not recognize you as Fletcher Colton, but they'll make you for a cop right away."

He glanced down at himself. "How? I'll hide my holster."

"It's not the gun," she said with another laugh.

"What then? How can I not pass as your assistant?"

"Do you dance?" she asked.

He grimaced.

And she laughed again. "Have you ever gone to a nightclub—" she held up a hand when he started to open his mouth "—that hasn't been a crime scene?"

"Not for a while," he admitted.

Her curiosity piqued again. She asked, "Why not?"

"I've been busy," he said. "With work, with my family."

She sighed. "I understand being busy, but in my business that's a good thing." It meant she was in high demand, that people wanted to come where she was spinning. "Not so much in your business."

He shook his head. "No. It's not. That's why I really need to catch the Slasher."

"And you're right, then, that you need my help," she said. He wasn't going to pass as her assistant without it. "Do you have anything in your closet that isn't khaki and or button-down?"

"I have jeans," he said.

She pointed at hers. "Like these?"

"I throw them out before they look like that," he said. But the way his gaze moved over her skin that the holes exposed, he didn't seem to mind that she hadn't.

She smiled and stepped closer to him and touched

the buttons on his chest. "And something that doesn't button down?"

"I will need the button down to hide my gun," he said.

"Hiding your gun is less important than hiding that you're a cop," she said. "Just your presence alone will scare the Slasher away."

Which wasn't a bad thing. She would rather not have another attack happen here. But she didn't want them to happen anywhere else either.

"I have to catch this person," he said. "Whoever it is, they're so dangerous. Their victims will be disfigured for life, and eventually…eventually…" His throat moved as he swallowed. "Someone is going to die."

Fear clutched her with the knowledge that he was right. Eventually someone was going to die. She didn't want that someone to be him, though.

Where was the news coverage? The Slasher scrolled through their phone, trying to pull up stories about the latest attack. But the only one that came up was the last one. In Salt Lake City.

Not this one in Conners, near Owl Creek, Idaho. The area was pretty.

With the lake and the river and the mountains in the distance. It was so idyllic that something bad happening here should have been big news.

Should have incited a panic.

And it had at the club. Once the victim had been found, everyone had been screaming and running in fear, afraid that they might be next.

And maybe they would be.

Because the Slasher was going to stick around town and make damn sure that Owl Creek acknowledged how powerful they were. And how very dangerous...

Chapter 7

Fletcher hadn't wanted to admit it, but Kiki was probably right about his ability to fit in at a nightclub. His cover wasn't going to be effective if *anyone* suspected he was a cop. Because rumors would spread, and nobody would talk to him.

And the Slasher would just move on to another nightclub and find their next victim elsewhere.

So he'd agreed to go shopping with Kiki for some clothes that would help him go undercover as her assistant. But first he'd stopped by the hospital in Conners to check on the Slasher's latest victim. Some of the guy's wounds had gotten infected, so he was receiving IV antibiotics. He also needed more surgeries to try to limit the scarring he was going to have.

The guy had a long road ahead of him to heal. Physically and emotionally. But when Fletcher walked up to his door, he heard laughter behind it. A man's and then a woman's familiar, raspy laugh. He pushed it open to find Kiki standing next to the man's bed, smiling down at him. Today she wore shorts so short that the bottoms of the pockets hung out of them, and a T-shirt that was so short that it showed off her belly button and the piercing in it.

Fletcher's pulse quickened.

Kiki glanced at him, and her smile faded. "I should leave now and let you get your rest."

The guy glanced at Fletcher, too, and emitted a soft sigh. "Don't think that's happening. Another cop with questions, I presume?"

Fletcher swallowed a groan and nodded. Kiki had been right about people pegging him for police. "I'm Detective Colton." He identified himself, flipping his badge out to show it. "I just have a few questions."

"I should go," Kiki said. "I have a date to go shopping with someone." She glanced at her wrist. "In just a little while."

"You have a date," the man said, and he didn't swallow his groan.

"You're engaged," Kiki reminded him.

"Yeah, but you came to visit me, and she hasn't."

"Are you two friends?" Fletcher asked. And if so, why hadn't Kiki mentioned that to him before?

"I wish," the guy replied. "Her helper never lets anyone through to talk to her."

"I just came to check on him," Kiki said, "after finding out what happened at the club."

"That damn Slasher…" the guy murmured, his voice cracking.

"Did you see them?" Fletcher asked.

"I just saw that damn blade coming toward my face and then…" He shuddered. "I didn't see anything."

"What were you doing in the alley?" Fletcher asked. "Why'd you go out there?"

The guy glanced at Kiki who stood near the door, and as if she'd realized he was reluctant to admit it in front of her, she waved and popped out of the room.

The guy groaned again. "It was stupid."

"What was? Why were you out there?"

"I found a note in my pocket. Someone must have shoved it in there on the dance floor. I thought…"

"What did the note say?"

"Meet me in the alley for some fun." The guy lifted one of his bandaged hands to his bandaged face. "Some fun…"

"Do you have the note?" Fletcher asked.

The guy shrugged. "I don't know. They took all my stuff when I got to the hospital."

It wasn't with his things. The techs had all that stuff now—had already processed it for DNA, fingerprints, whatever they could find to help find the Slasher.

"We'll keep looking for it," Fletcher assured him.

"I hope you find it before my fiancée does." His voice cracked again with fear. "Oh, God, maybe she already found it and that's why she hasn't been here."

Fletcher doubted that, but he would check with her, too. "She wasn't at the club?"

"No, it was my bachelor party. We just stopped in

because we knew the DJ was hot." He glanced toward that closed door, as if trying to see her through the solid wood.

"You came there for Kiki?" Fletcher asked.

The guy nodded. "A lot of people follow her around the club circuit. She's good."

"And hot," Fletcher added.

The guy chuckled a bit, then flinched, wrinkling the bandages on his face.

"You need your rest," Fletcher told him. "But please, if you think of anything you haven't already shared—"

"I know," the guy replied. "I know. I should have told the police everything."

"That was it?" Fletcher asked, double-checking.

"Just the note," the guy replied. "That was it. I didn't mention it before because I didn't want my fiancée to know."

But since she wasn't the woman who'd visited him right now, Fletcher had a feeling she'd already figured it out even without the note being found with his stuff.

Where was the note?

"Hope you heal quickly," Fletcher told him before turning to reach for the door that had closed behind Kiki such a short while ago.

"I got a question for you, Detective," the guy said.

Fletcher looked back over his shoulder. "What?"

"Why?" the guy asked. "Why me? Why would anyone do this?"

Fletcher shook his head. "I don't know. But I'm going to work hard to get those answers for you and the other victims and to put this person away."

Tears rolled down the guy's face, wetting his bandages.

And Fletcher felt a jab to his heart. The guy hadn't been a great fiancé, but he hadn't deserved this.

Nobody did.

Fletcher opened the door, and he felt that jab to his heart again. But this was for another reason, for the woman leaning against the wall across from him.

She was definitely hot.

And Fletcher couldn't help but think, as he stepped into the hall to join her, that this undercover assignment was going to be far more dangerous than he'd ever considered. And not just because of the Slasher.

Kiki fought the smirk that was trying to curl up her lips. "Hey, what's keeping you?" she called from her place outside the door of the men's dressing room.

Since there was only one clerk in the store, and she was planted behind the register, Kiki had been playing sales associate, picking clothes for Fletcher to try on. After meeting up at the hospital in Conners, Fletcher had followed her to the outlet mall there since all the shops in Owl Creek were a bit higher end. The outlet mall was cheaper with a wider variety of stores—so many that this one wasn't at all busy. They were also the only customers in the store, so nobody would mistakenly think she was calling out to them. Fletcher should also have no doubt that he was the one she was talking to, yet he wasn't replying. Or coming out.

"Fletcher!"

"What's keeping me?" the question bounced back at her from the dressing room. "I can barely move in these pants." He pushed open the door and stepped out, wearing the skintight jeans and silk shirt she'd picked for him. The emerald green made his eyes sparkle even more and the silk molded to his chest and arms like the denim molded to his legs.

"It's either go for this look or the tattoos and piercings," she said. "That's what Troy looks like."

"I'm looking *for* Troy. I don't want to look *like* him," Fletcher said.

"You don't want to look like a cop," she reminded him.

He raised his fingers to his lips, trying to shush her like his undercover assignment had already started.

She laughed and pointed at the teenage clerk. "She has earbuds in."

He relaxed a bit, and when he did, the seams of the shirt strained at his broad shoulders and along his arms. To be built like that, he had to work out. A lot. The guys Kiki knew who worked out like that usually wore clothes to show off the result of their efforts, not hide them.

"You need some better fitting clothes," she insisted.

He reached for the top button of the shirt. "Yeah, and these aren't it."

"They fit better than your usual clothes," she pointed out, "which look like they're two sizes too big."

"I have to be able to run in case I have to chase a suspect down, and I need to be able to hide my weapon."

"Not everybody in the club hides their weapons," Kiki said. "If they have a permit to carry, some bouncers let them in with them."

Fletcher groaned. "Alcohol and guns. What could go wrong?"

"The Slasher isn't shooting their victims," Kiki said. "And not everybody that comes into the club drinks. Some just come for the music."

"Not the Slasher."

"You don't even know if that person comes inside the club. Maybe they just wait out in the alley until someone steps out for a smoke break or something."

He shook his head and glanced toward that clerk again. The girl wasn't even looking their way. She was focused on whatever video was playing on her phone. And nobody else had come into the store yet. "The Slasher doesn't wait for their victims to come to them."

Kiki tensed with dread. "But I've never seen anyone getting attacked like that happening inside." Fights. Sure. There were often fights. Sometimes someone even waved around a gun that Fletcher, with good reason, seemed to disapprove of them carrying while they were clubbing.

"Most of the victims have admitted to getting a note slipped into their pocket without them even realizing it." He tried to shove his hand into the pocket of his jeans, but they were too tight for him to fit more than his fingertips inside. "These aren't going to allow for that."

So he wanted the Slasher to slip him a note? To try to lure him into an alley?

She resisted the urge to shiver as a sudden chill chased down her spine. He wasn't just going under-cover then. He was setting himself up as bait. She'd agreed to let him act like her assistant as his cover, but she hadn't realized how dangerous it was going to be. And she really didn't want him getting hurt like that man she'd visited in the hospital earlier today.

"And I thought it was cool to wear baggy pants and flannel jackets right now," he persisted.

She smiled at his persistence and his language. "Cool?"

"Hip, fly, whatever the words are that you kids use nowadays," he said, his green eyes twinkling with amusement.

"So are you trying to sound like my grandfather?" she asked, her smile widening. "Because he sounds more hip and fly than you do." And a giggle slipped out. "But then I guess you are older than I am." Probably five years at the most, but she couldn't help but tease him.

He glared at her, but his eyes were still twinkling. "I am not that old. I am just not that…"

"Cool?" she asked. He certainly wasn't now. Not in those clothes. He was *hot*, and she was getting hot as he undid another button and revealed some of the dark hair on his chest. Her heart beat faster and faster. Then she took a step back and whirled around. "I'll get you some hoodies and other things so you can hide your weapon."

But she wasn't necessarily talking about his gun. His weapon was how damn sexy he was.

He chuckled as if he'd realized he'd affected her. But maybe that was only fair. She'd purposely worn a pair of her shortest shorts just to get to him.

When she came back with an armload of hoodies and flannels and some looser jeans and Timberlands, he opened the door to his dressing room. The clerk hadn't even looked up from her phone while Kiki had flitted around the store picking out more clothes for Fletcher to try on. She wasn't paying any attention to them at all.

And Kiki kind of wished she was because she had no excuse not to step inside the dressing room with Fletcher to dump her armload onto the bench behind him. But when she would have ducked out again, he stepped between her and the door.

"What did you bring me now? Jeans I'm going to have to lie down on the floor to get on?" he asked.

She chuckled. "Bed. People usually lie down on the bed to get their jeans on. But for me." She patted her hips. "It's easier to get them on if I bounce up and down while I'm standing." And when she bounced to demonstrate, his gaze slipped down her body again.

A groan slipped through his lips. "Wouldn't you rather go shopping for you?" he asked.

"No. This is fun. And I already have all the clothes I need for the club." She kept a separate wardrobe of things that fit with the brand she'd built as a stylish and trendy female DJ whose music got people moving. "You need something you can wear this weekend, something that will help you fit in with the club scene."

He rolled his eyes.

"You really don't like clubs?" she asked.

"What's to like? They're loud and hot and crowded and really damn dangerous lately."

She couldn't deny that, not after she'd checked in on the Slasher's latest victim at the hospital. "That's why you need to fit in," she said. "If you want to catch the…"

She glanced around him to where that clerk stood at the register, watching her phone. The buds were still in her ears. "Slasher."

Fletcher walked toward the pile of clothes she'd dumped on the bench. "What do you want me to try on next? And why do I feel like a life-size Barbie doll right now?"

"Ken," she corrected him. Then shook her head and corrected herself, "G.I. Joe."

"That's my brother Wade," Fletcher said with a sigh of his own. Wade had been hurt, badly, on his last deployment, so it was no wonder that Fletcher was probably worried about him. His whole family had to be.

"How is he doing?" Kiki asked.

"He's healing," Fletcher said, his voice a little gruff with emotion.

He clearly loved his family very much.

"It was sweet of you to check on the Slasher's latest victim," he said, his green gaze fixed on her with that unnerving intensity.

"I feel bad it happened while I was spinning, and I never noticed…" That someone was getting disfigured while she played. There had been so many bandages on the man, so much pain in his face. She shuddered.

"The music is loud. The place is crowded. There's no way you would have noticed," Fletcher said.

She was touched that he was defending her or at least trying to make her feel a little less guilty that someone had been hurt while she'd been playing.

"So how is this cover going to work for you so that you'll notice what's going on?" she asked.

"Do I have to stick by you all the time or just help with setup and takedown of your equipment?"

"Setup and takedown only," she assured him. "Troy only hung out with me for a couple of songs, usually. We had a little dance thing." She smiled as she considered teaching it to Fletcher.

He shook his head and backed up. "No dancing."

"Nobody will guess you're a cop if you do," she assured him.

He shook his head and some of his hair fell across his eyes. "I should get this cut," he grumbled as he shoved it off his face.

"No!" she gasped, and she reached up to put her hands in it as if the scissors were heading toward it as he spoke. His hair was so soft that her skin tingled from contact with it. "This is the one thing that makes you look less like a cop."

"You say that like it's a bad thing to look like a cop," he said.

"If you want this undercover thing to get the results you want, it is a bad thing," she pointed out. "Otherwise..."

"Otherwise what?" he asked.

"I have no problem with the way you look," she admitted, and she knew she should pull her hands from his hair, but it was just so soft. And he was so good looking with his chiseled features and vivid green eyes.

His mouth curved into a slight grin. "Really?"

Standing in that dressing room with him, trapped between the bench and his long, muscular body, she might have felt a little uneasy. But she didn't particularly want to escape right now. She enjoyed flirting with him entirely too much. And touching him.

"Well…" she murmured. "There is one thing that you could use…"

And he arched a dark brow over one eye. "Are you going to suggest a tattoo or a piercing again?"

She shook her head. "No. What you could really use…" And she leaned a little closer to him, her mouth near his ear, her chest almost touching his.

His body tensed, and he audibly sucked in a breath. "What?" he asked, his voice a rasp.

"You could really use—" she said, her voice all breathy "—an iron."

He chuckled. "Is that why you're picking out all tight clothes for me?" he asked. "So there will be no wrinkles?"

She glanced down his body the way he'd glanced down hers. He still wore those tight jeans, molded to his muscular thighs. "Yeah, that's the reason…" she said with a laugh, her particularly naughty-sounding laugh.

"Are you flirting with me, Ms. Shelton?" he asked.

"Don't take it personally," she advised him. "I flirt with everyone. Occupational hazard."

He laughed. "I'll try to remember that."

And she would have to try to remember that he was only helping her out as part of his cover in the club. He didn't really want to spend this time with her. He just wanted to catch the Slasher.

Chapter 8

Club Ignition was just outside the city limits of Owl Creek in what had once been an abandoned warehouse. It was all metal and brick with a big open ceiling. And it was also loud and hot and crowded with sweaty bodies. All the things Fletcher hated about nightclubs.

But there was also Kiki.

She lit up the place, shining brighter than the strobe lights flashing around the club. One flashed now, nearly blinding him. How the hell was he supposed to spot any potential suspects when he could barely see at all?

The lights kept rhythm with the music, flashing in time to the beat. So not only was she managing the sound, but the light show, too.

And the sound, while loud, was also rich. Thick and heavy like cream and just as smooth. How did she do it all? He'd had no idea how much was involved with being a DJ. In addition to the expense of buying and maintaining all the equipment, there was also the physical labor of moving and unpacking the equipment. But the work didn't end with setup or takedown.

In addition to the lights, she also worked four turntables, mixing songs and adjusting bass, and as she turned and mixed, she moved. Her body swayed to the slower songs, jumped to the faster ones and Fletcher wasn't the only one who couldn't look away from her.

Everybody in the club was as fascinated as he was. The men tried to get close to her, but she had a short barricade separating her DJ booth from the crowd. Knowing Kiki like he was starting to, she probably used it more to protect her equipment than herself.

But whatever her reasoning was, Fletcher was glad she had it, that she wasn't vulnerable to that crowd that could include the Slasher. Or just some men that might not respect her boundaries.

Even a group of women jumped up and down near that barricade, screaming her name with excitement on their flushed faces. "Kiki! Kiki! Play our song!"

Despite the headphones she wore, she must have heard them. Because when the song "Where My Girls At" started pumping out of the speakers, those women lost their minds, screaming louder and jumping up and down even higher, their arms waving wildly over their heads.

He'd planted himself near the booth, but closer to the floor so he could watch it. Too close to the floor, because one of the women from that group tried pulling him out with them to dance. He shook his head.

"Come on, Fletcher!" Kiki called out to him over her microphone. "Dance with my girls!"

"Then you gotta dance with us, Kiki!" a guy yelled out, pointing to the floor.

"With me!" another guy yelled.

As the men hollered at her, and she ignored them or just shook her head, the women tugged Fletcher out onto that floor. He knew how to dance; he'd grown up with three younger sisters who'd needed practice partners for prom and other school dances. But those dances had been a while ago, so he didn't know how to do half the stuff these women were doing.

Even then, he might have stayed out on the floor if he'd thought it would give the Slasher an opportunity to slip a note in his pocket. But while the women were rubbing up against him and touching him, he didn't feel anything being put inside his pockets. And given the damage to the victims, he wasn't sure that a woman could have inflicted it.

Some of the victims had been big guys. Wouldn't they have been able to fight off a woman?

No. It was more likely a man who'd done the damage. A left-handed man, according to the medical examiner who'd studied the wounds of all the victims. So he studied the guys who called out to Kiki, wondering if it was one of them.

And he broke away from the women and leaped over the barricade to join Kiki in her booth that was already overcrowded with equipment. If he was going to dance with anyone, it was going to be her. Hell, he'd rather do more than dance with her.

But he was here to find a killer.

Not a good time.

Fletcher could dance. First with the women.

She would have been concerned that he was getting a note slipped in one of his pockets, but she knew those women well. They really were her girls. They came out to the clubs because they loved to dance.

"You've been holding out on me," Kiki said when he joined her in the booth. "Making it sound like you didn't even know how to…"

"I never said I couldn't. Just that I don't because I don't want to," he explained. But he was moving with her, against her, grinding up on her.

Instead of being offended, she giggled. And she'd thought he was uptight.

Fletcher Colton was full of surprises. And damn, he looked good. He wore a tight white T-shirt that changed color with every flash of the strobe lights. To hide his holster and his weapon, over the T-shirt he wore a light checked button-down shirt, but she had insisted that he leave it unbuttoned. And he had.

The jeans were loose and baggy but with enough holes to show off the hair on his muscular legs. And to make her heart race a little every time she looked at him. Or felt that brush of hair against her bare legs. She wore leather again, but shorts and a vest. And instead of black, she wore red—nearly the same color of the tips of her hair that swung around her shoulders as she danced.

Music filled her. Lifted her.

It had always been like that, ever since she was a little kid. She moved to it as if it was inside her, guiding her arms and legs. Her heart thumped in perfect tempo with the beat, just as heavy and deep. Except for now.

With Fletcher dancing with her.

Now her heart beat faster and faster with every touch of his body against hers.

She twirled in his arms and leaned close to his ear, whispering, "Aren't you supposed to be investigating?"

"I'm making sure my cover works," Fletcher said, grinning as if he knew how badly he was getting to her.

How much he was making her want him.

Like in the dressing room earlier this week, when she'd touched his hair and had wanted to keep on touching it. She'd touched it earlier when he'd showed up at the club to help her unload the equipment. She'd put some mousse in it, played with it, all on the pretext of making him look the part of her assistant.

Troy had never looked like this. While some women had probably found him attractive and danced with him, the crowd hadn't reacted to him like they had Fletcher.

And, while she had danced with other people before, she hadn't reacted to anyone like she was reacting to dancing with Fletcher. Because she wanted to do more than dance.

Her heart pounded so hard that she struggled to breathe. She needed air and some distance from her sexy assistant. "You can man the turntables while I take a bathroom break, then," she told him.

"What?" His green eyes widened with shock and fear.

She wasn't really leaving him to play anything, she explained. She'd already put a set of songs in order, including the requests from some bachelor party attendees. The music would keep pumping from the speakers while she caught the breath she'd lost, that her lungs ached to find again.

She wasn't out of breath from the dancing or from the spinning but from the closeness of Fletcher Colton. Of how he looked and of how he made her feel…

So damn attracted to him.

She slipped past him and down the couple of steps to the barricade that she vaulted herself over. As she moved through the crowd, guys called out to her and tried to dance with her like Fletcher had been. But she didn't stop moving until she pushed her way into the crowded bathroom.

Women moved aside and applauded while they chattered at and around her.

"Kiki, you're the best!"

"Kiki, what a huge improvement over Troy."

"I liked Troy."

"Yeah, we know why."

"Who is he?" one of her usual crew asked. Claire was a blonde who always wore bright red lipstick.

"He's hot!" Janie said. Her hair was dark like Kiki's but wildly curly, even a little frizzy tonight—probably from the heat.

"He yours?" Amy asked. She was a redhead, but probably about as natural a redhead as the tips of Kiki's hair were natural.

Kiki's pulse quickened even more at the thought of that. Of Fletcher being hers.

But she didn't want anyone. Not really. At least not for keeps. That would make life too complicated. She was committed to traveling from club to club, building her brand so that she could get a record deal like so many other DJs she knew.

She shook her head. "He's just an old friend."

Janie snorted. "Looks like more than that."

"Is he?" Amy asked with a trace of disappointment.

Feeling a pang of jealousy that these women were so interested in Fletcher, she smiled slightly, smugly, as if she was claiming him. "Now, ladies, I need to use the bathroom so I can get back to the turntables."

As she slipped into a stall, voices called out to her, requesting songs. Someday, maybe, the song they requested would be one of hers.

That was the dream, one she'd had since she was a little girl and had felt that music moving inside her. But the music wasn't the only thing inside her tonight.

Tonight, she had that overwhelming attraction to Fletcher. And all these women talking about him, drooling over him, only made him more attractive to her. As if he hadn't already been attractive enough.

But he was only here because of the case. She had to remind herself of that, of the Slasher. Detective Fletcher Colton wasn't here to dance with her or to drive her to distraction over how damn attractive she found him.

He was here to catch someone before that person hurt anyone else. That was what mattered most. Making sure nobody else got hurt, or worse.

A little flicker of fear shortened her breath for a moment as she worried that she might be the one getting hurt if she wasn't careful. Not by the Slasher.

But by Fletcher, if she acted on this attraction she felt for him. She couldn't do that for so many reasons. She had her friendship with his sister Ruby, her busy schedule, her life goals...

Their careers were going to take them in different directions. His was going to take him into dangerous places.

And she'd already lost people she'd loved. She couldn't fall for Fletcher.

The Slasher needed another victim. The police wouldn't be able to keep another attack from the media. Wouldn't be able to keep the story from spreading, from going national like the other attacks had.

The Slasher needed another victim because they needed the attention, the fear, the respect.

So they were at their usual hunting ground. A crowded club.

There were so many men to choose from.

Even Kiki had brought someone new tonight.

Someone to help her with the equipment. Or was he her boyfriend? The way they'd danced together, the way they'd looked at each other...

They definitely knew each other well. There was an

intimacy between them. If not, the Slasher would have been concerned that this man was something else...

Like a police officer.

Would one go undercover to catch the Slasher?

Were they that important?

How many different police departments and agencies were trying to catch them?

Trying to stop them?

Nothing and nobody would. And if anyone tried to get in their way...

They would wind up being the next victim of the Slasher, and maybe that person would lose more than their looks.

Maybe they would lose their life...

Chapter 9

Fletcher wanted nothing to do with the turntables or with all the requests being shouted at him while Kiki was gone. Where had she gone? Just the restroom?

Not the alley.

His pulse quickened as he thought of that—of her becoming a victim of the Slasher. The serial attacker hadn't gone after women before, but that didn't mean that the person wouldn't, especially if Kiki stepped into the alley at the wrong moment. As he started across the dance floor toward the bar and the door behind it through which they'd dragged all her equipment, he got distracted by the sound of a familiar, raspy voice.

"Let go of me," Kiki said with indignation and determination.

"You danced with that loser but you won't dance

with me?" The man sounded indignant as well. "It's my bachelor party. Come on."

"I know, and I've been playing your favorite songs," Kiki replied. "And to keep doing that, I need to get back to my booth."

"Just one dance. Or a drink. I'll buy you a drink. I can buy you a lot of things, pretty Kiki."

"I am not for sale," she said. "Now let me go!"

"Let her go!" Fletcher growled as he pushed through to where some guy, just a little taller than Kiki, was holding tightly to one of her bare arms.

Kiki tried wrestling free, but the man's grip tightened to the point her skin was turning red.

"Oh, here's your lapdog now," the guy remarked with a disparaging smirk. "Come on, Kiki, give up losers like this for real men. Men with means."

"I don't—"

Fletcher didn't interrupt her. He just grabbed the man and jerked his arm behind his back so that it fell away from hers. With the abrupt release, she stumbled back a step into the crowd that had gathered around them.

The guy wrestled in Fletcher's grasp. "How dare you! Get your hands off me!"

"I will break your arm," he threatened. He raised the man's arm a little higher behind his back until he cried out. "Don't you ever touch her again."

"Let me go!" the guy said again, but it was more of a frightened whine than the condescending demand it had been earlier.

Fletcher twisted the guy's arm just a little harder before he released him. The minute he did, the guy swung his fist toward him. Fletcher ducked and swung back, striking him just enough to knock him into the man's friends who'd gathered behind them. "Now get the hell out."

Finally, the bouncers arrived, dragging the man from the crowd, as he hurled insults and protestations. "This is my bachelor party! Do you know who I am?"

Nobody cared. The mocking laughter of the crowd followed the guy out along with a few of his friends.

"You're going to be sorry!" was his last pitiful proclamation.

The laughter got louder.

Nobody was.

But the way Kiki looked at Fletcher, glaring as she rushed past him toward her booth, he figured he might be sorry later when she had time to talk to him. What had she wanted him to do? Let the guy hurt her?

The thought wrenched his guts, making him feel sick. While she might have been annoyed with him, nobody else was. They all patted his back and shoulders. "Way to protect Kiki!"

"Let me buy you a drink," someone offered, and he was swept up with the crowd gathered around the bar until he was up against the long peninsula of granite and glass.

"Drink's on me," the bartender said when cards and money were extended toward him.

"Just coffee," Fletcher told him. He couldn't drink on the job, especially this job. He needed to be alert to deal with the Slasher. And if he had alcohol, tired as he was, he wouldn't be able to stay awake. Unless he watched Kiki.

"Everybody, get back on the floor!" Kiki's command echoed from the speakers. "I need you all out here. I need you to…" Her voice trailed off, replaced with the upbeat music and song, "Dance, dance, dance!"

The clubgoers shrieked and headed back out, jumping and yelling along with the lyrics. With Kiki.

She wanted the drama involving her forgotten. She wanted to focus on the music, on other people having a good time. That seemed very important to her.

The bartender leaned over the bar, that was a whole lot less crowded now, and said, "Thanks for getting rid of that entitled ass. Too many rich guys come in here thinking they can have whatever they want."

Fletcher focused on the bartender. With dark blond hair and stubble on his pointy chin, he was probably a little younger than Fletcher—maybe late twenties, like Kiki's age. But there was a jadedness to him already, despite his youth.

"Must get sickening," Fletcher agreed with him. "Having to listen to them spout off about how important they are."

The bartender nodded. "You have no idea. Just because they have money, they think they can treat everybody like dirt." He snorted. "Money doesn't buy class or manners, that's for damn sure."

Fletcher was glad that when he'd met the bartender earlier that evening, when he and Kiki had been bringing in her equipment, he hadn't shared his last name. Thanks to his dad's real estate investments, the Coltons had money. Fortunately, thanks to how their mom had raised them, they also had class and manners.

But this guy seemed to lump all rich people together and equate them with rudeness and entitlement. He'd probably had some bad experiences over the years, but it looked like his bitterness about rich guys ran pretty deep.

Had all the Slasher's victims had money?

Fletcher made a mental note to follow up on that. Wanting to show camaraderie with his new acquaintance, he grinned and picked up the mug of coffee. "Thanks," he said. "And cheers to getting rid of entitled jerks!"

The bartender grinned.

"Cheers," another voice chimed in.

Fletcher glanced down the bar to where an older man sat alone, his glass lifted toward Fletcher. With iron gray hair and several deep lines in his face, this guy had to be in his sixties. He didn't look like the other clubgoers. Maybe he owned the place.

Fletcher leaned across the bar and asked the bartender, "What's his story? Owner?"

The bartender snorted. "No. Just a regular customer. He comes around a lot."

"Really?" Fletcher asked. The guy didn't seem to be into the music, but he kept looking at the dance floor.

"Yeah, I thought he was a cop at first, but he's actually just a dad looking for his missing daughter."

A pang of sympathy for the distraught father struck Fletcher. "Oh…"

"Yeah, sucks. He hasn't seen her for a few years.

Don't know why he thinks he's going to just happen to run into her in a club someday." He shrugged. "But whatever…"

"Bart! Bart!" a male customer called from the end of the bar.

"Gotta go," Bart said. "Don't wanna keep these entitled jerks waiting."

When the bartender walked away, Fletcher approached the older guy. "Cheers," he said to him again.

Unlike the bartender, who wore a black uniform that was fading to gray from age and frequent washing, this guy wore a suit that looked tailored and expensive. He also wore an expensive watch on his right hand, which probably made him a lefty. He could have been one of the entitled jerks that Bart and Fletcher had been talking about.

Hell, with the shares of Colton Properties that Fletcher had just inherited, he could probably be one of those entitled jerks. But he hadn't even stuck around for the reading of the will to find out what the value of those shares were. It had been too hard.

Losing someone sucked.

"Cheers," the stranger repeated. "Better enjoy your drink because I think you're in a little bit of trouble."

"How's that?" Fletcher asked. "Think that guy is going to call the police?" It would be funny if he did.

But Fletcher didn't want to blow his cover.

"Kiki doesn't seem too happy with you," the guy said with a slight grin.

Fletcher groaned. "Yeah."

"She can take care of herself."

The way she'd whirled on him with that pepper spray last weekend, she'd proved that she could. But with the Slasher on the loose...

And the way that jerk had been squeezing her arm...

She would probably have bruises, and that infuriated Fletcher. "I actually showed some restraint," Fletcher insisted. He hadn't thrown the first punch, and he hadn't broken the guy's arm like he'd been tempted to for hurting Kiki.

The man chuckled. "I doubt Kiki's going to see it that way, especially since it was the guy's bachelor party."

"So, you know Kiki pretty well," Fletcher remarked. And he also paid a lot of attention to what was going on in the club since he'd known that the guy who'd hit on her was the guest of honor at his bachelor party. Was this stranger so observant just because he was looking for his daughter?

The guy shook his head. "No, I don't know Kiki all that well. I've just been at some clubs while she's playing the music."

He definitely wasn't part of the club scene, despite how often he must frequent them. Fletcher could relate.

"You haven't been with her before," the gentleman observed. "She usually has some skinny, tattooed guy with her. Where's he tonight?"

Fletcher shrugged. "Good question. He took off on her last weekend and hasn't been seen since."

Fletcher saw him flinch and regretted that he'd probably reminded the older man of his missing daughter. Had she run away from home? Was that how he'd lost track of her?

Fletcher wanted to ask these questions, but appearing too interested would risk his cover, too. He narrowed his eyes and studied the guy. "Are you a cop?" he asked.

The man grimaced. "No. I don't have much use for the police."

"Why's that?" Fletcher asked.

The stranger sighed. "They don't give some things, some people, the attention they deserve."

The Slasher was all about getting attention, but Fletcher hadn't been able to figure out why yet. Was this it? Because the man wasn't getting the help he wanted to find his daughter?

"I'm sorry," Fletcher said.

"Why?" the man asked, narrowing his blue eyes. "Are you a cop?"

Ignoring the jab of concern that he had risked his cover, he laughed heartily. "That's funny," he said. "Me? A cop?"

"So then you're more like her other assistant?" the man asked.

And Fletcher wondered now if the man was looking for his daughter or for drugs. "No. I'm nothing like Troy either," he assured him. "Kiki and I are old friends. I just stepped in to help her out."

Until the Slasher was caught.

And Fletcher needed that to happen soon, before anyone else got hurt. Or worse.

Kiki should have been relieved that Fletcher stayed away from her booth. She was annoyed that he'd felt the need to step into that situation on the dance floor.

Like she'd needed his help.

Like he thought she couldn't take care of herself.

She'd been handling jerks like that for a long time on her own. She knew how to get rid of them. A few sharp words cut up their egos like the Slasher.

No. Nothing compared to what the Slasher did to their victims. Nothing.

She couldn't get over the sight of the victim she'd visited in the hospital. And she hadn't seen him until after he'd been treated. She couldn't imagine what Troy must have seen when he'd found that victim in the alley behind that Salt Lake City club. No wonder he'd taken off when he'd heard about another attack.

Though apparently, he had other reasons to avoid the authorities. She felt a pang of guilt over that, over helping him evade his responsibilities. But she'd had no idea he had children. And just because he was a dead-beat dad, it didn't make him the Slasher like Fletcher clearly suspected he was.

But why?

What would his motive have been?

What was the Slasher's motive for hurting people so horrifically? For disfiguring them like that?

She shivered despite the warmth of the crowded club. And she tried to peer through that mob of people to catch sight of Fletcher.

Where had he gone?

Was he still wrestling with that creep who'd hit on her? Or was he wrestling with someone far more dangerous? Trying to get a better view, she climbed onto one of the speakers in the booth. She danced along with the music she played while searching the crowd.

She caught sight of him, his dark hair mussed despite the mousse she'd put in it for him—or maybe because of it, since she'd kept playing with the soft strands. Or had one of the women who'd danced with Fletcher messed it up? Or maybe it had happened during his tussle with that boor of a bachelor who had acted like his money could get him whatever he wanted from any woman.

She snorted at the thought. She would play song requests, but those were the only requests she fulfilled. And most everyone who came to her shows knew that.

Did Fletcher know that? And if he did, why hadn't he let her handle that creep on her own?

She'd done it plenty of times. She hadn't asked for his help. She didn't need him, but she damn well wanted him. He was so attractive.

From her vantage point on her speaker, she peered around the club, trying to find him. He was at the bar talking to Mr. Sullivan. She'd met the guy a couple of years ago, and every time she saw him, her heart ached for his sadness and desperation.

He'd shown her a picture of his daughter, asking if Kiki had seen her. If she had, she wouldn't have recognized her as the girl wearing a school uniform, her hair pulled back into a tight ponytail. If Kiki had ever seen her, the girl had probably looked like so many others who hung around the clubs, desperate to have a good time.

Some were a little too desperate.

Desperate to look older, prettier, more desirable. So desperate that they sometimes made bad choices. Kiki didn't know for sure if that was what had happened to Dan Sullivan's daughter any more than she knew for certain if she'd ever seen her before.

She'd disappointed the older man because she couldn't help him. Fletcher could. But was that why he was at the bar talking to the man?

Or did he wonder if he was the Slasher, just like he'd suspected Troy, too?

Fletcher's head turned from the bar toward her. Across that crowded room, she couldn't see his eyes, but she could feel the intensity of his gaze.

That look he'd been giving her every time they came into contact. Lately, they'd connected a little too often for unfortunate reasons.

His father's funeral.

The attack at the club in Conners.

But every time they saw each other, they had this bizarre connection. He found her as attractive as she found him. But neither of them could afford a distraction right now, not with that dangerous attacker out there, probably prowling clubs for another victim.

Was that Fletcher's real reason for going undercover at the club? Not just to find clues to the Slasher's identity but to get the Slasher to try to attack him?

He'd wanted the loose jeans—loose enough to chase after a suspect, but also loose enough for a note to be slipped into his pocket.

That was why she'd been so desperate to find him in

the crowd. To make sure he was still inside the club and not out in the alley.

Because ever since their shopping trip, she'd had the horrible feeling that Fletcher was using himself as bait for this vicious person. That he was setting himself up to be the Slasher's next victim.

Chapter 10

Fletcher had avoided Kiki since he'd saved her from that drunk because, like the man at the bar, Fletcher doubted that was how she'd seen it. That he'd saved her.

She probably just figured he'd interfered. And he had no doubt that he would hear about it when the night was over, and when he was alone with her. Despite knowing he would probably get told off, he couldn't wait for the night to end. And not just so that he could be alone with her.

He was so damn tired. It wasn't for lack of sleep. He was used to working late, sometimes even around the clock, when he had a case to solve. He was tired because of the noise and the music and the definite attraction he felt for Kiki.

She was amazing.

The way she worked all that complicated equipment left him in awe. The sounds she made...

Especially when she sang along with some of the lyrics. Her voice was amazing. Sexy and vibrant and hauntingly beautiful. Just like her.

When she danced, she moved like the music was inside her, pouring out of her every pore. She was so captivating it was nearly impossible to look away from her. Like everybody else in the club, he watched her now, dancing away behind the turntables.

She'd even been on top of one of the speakers earlier tonight. As if she'd been looking for him—and maybe she had been, because once their gazes had met, she'd jumped down. And he'd felt a little flicker of excitement that she might have been concerned about him.

With the way she kept distracting him, just by being her, how the hell was he going to catch the Slasher?

Sure, he'd been working, subtly interviewing that distraught father and the bartender. He'd gotten Dan Sullivan's name and his daughter's name. Caitlin.

He'd gotten the bartender's full name, too. Bart Taylor. Fletcher had even managed to sneak one of the glasses the man had touched beneath his shirt and then into the duffel bag he had slipped in with Kiki's equipment. He would run it for prints. Check out the man's past.

Find out why he hated rich guys so damn much.

If only the Slasher had ever left prints at the scene—something to match them to. But while several prints had been found at every scene, in every alley, none of them had been the same. The wounds and the weapon that had made them had all matched, though, so the Slasher must be just one solitary person committing every assault.

A left-handed person. A coroner had studied the wounds and determined that from the depth and direction of the cuts, a left-handed person had swung the blade.

The bartender was left-handed.

So was Dan Sullivan.

Fletcher hadn't realized there were so many left-handed people until he'd started looking for them in the club. The bartender and Sullivan hadn't been the only ones. The way other patrons had waved at the bartender to order drinks or some of the women had waved at Fletcher to draw his attention had shown they were probably left-handed, too.

What about Troy?

Kiki's former assistant was still high on his list of suspects. Where was he? The bartender had mentioned to Fletcher that he'd thought he'd seen him earlier. Someone else had said the same, but Fletcher had searched the crowd and hadn't caught any sight of him. He'd even searched the alley, too. Hell, he'd made a point of going out there at least once an hour to see if the Slasher was lying in wait for someone.

Or if they'd already attacked.

Did Kiki have any idea where her assistant was? She hadn't even known the guy's last name, or about his drug possession charge and back child support. Fletcher doubted she knew anything else about the man that would help locate him. But maybe she would know if he was left-handed or not.

If she would talk to him…

So far all she'd done was glare at him since he'd pulled that drunk off her on the dance floor.

Fletcher had wanted to check on her, to see if her arm had bruised from how tightly the guy had been gripping it. But the one time he'd gotten close, when he'd slipped that glass into his duffel bag, she'd given him such a look, all tight lips and lowered brows.

He was probably in more danger from her than from the Slasher right now. Nobody had tried to slip him a note. His pockets were empty. And the night was nearly over.

No. The night was over. It was early morning now.

Kiki had shouted "last call" and the songs were winding down in tempo while the lights gradually got brighter.

And the crowd thinned out.

Dan Sullivan had left a while ago.

The bartender had slipped away after fulfilling the last call orders. He was probably in the back, washing dirty glasses. Or maybe looking for one.

No. He wouldn't miss the one that Fletcher had tucked into his duffel bag. He wished he'd managed to get Dan Sullivan's glass, too, but the guy had only had one drink and he'd kept his hands around it the whole night, as if he'd been worried that someone would slip something in it.

Was that what he'd thought happened to his daughter?

While Fletcher had gotten him talking about his daughter, the man had just showed him his picture and said that she'd always liked going to nightclubs, even when she wasn't really old enough to get in.

So maybe he blamed nightclubs for her going missing. And the attacks on clubgoers was his way of getting revenge.

Because the viciousness of those attacks made them feel so personal.

Like someone was after something.

Notoriety or revenge?

Or both?

Fletcher sighed, which turned into a yawn so big that he closed his eyes and leaned against the barricade he'd been standing near, just outside Kiki's booth.

"Hey, old man, try to stay awake," Kiki chastised him, her voice soft and close to his ear.

Realizing that her voice was the only sound he heard but for a buzzing echo, he opened his eyes and blinked against the brightness of the lights. "Is it over?" he asked, letting his eagerness slip out. Maybe it hadn't been the eventful night he'd hoped it would be, but while he hadn't had a note slipped in his pocket, he had found some more potential suspects. Besides Troy.

The bartender had mentioned seeing him in the club, but when Fletcher had looked around, he hadn't seen anyone who'd matched the description he'd had of the man. Had he been there? Maybe he'd intended to help Kiki after all.

And then he'd seen Fletcher. Too bad Fletcher hadn't seen him.

"Yes, it's over," Kiki said, "and I have a lot of equip-

ment you need to help carry out, since you're so helpful and all…"

Fletcher flinched. "I figured I would pay for that."

"For making a scene? For embarrassing me?"

"The scene was already being made," he said. "That
guy was a jerk."

"He was drunk and acting like a bigshot in front
of his friends," she said. "It was his bachelor party."

"That doesn't give him the right to harass you,"
Fletcher said, appalled. "I'm glad I decided long ago
to never get married."

"You don't want to get married?" she asked.

He shook his head. His parents had not had the ideal
marriage. He wasn't sure if it was just because of how
much his dad had always worked but knowing how his
own relationships hadn't withstood his work schedule, he wasn't going to risk anything more permanent.
"Nope. And really, I don't think that guy should either.
What a dick."

Those lips, which had been tightly drawn together,
twitched up into a smile. "Yeah, he was, but I would
have handled him so that I didn't ruin his evening."

"I doubt his evening was ruined. I'm sure he went
on to another bar," Fletcher assured her. "Or maybe a
strip club."

She sighed. "He did kind of act like that was where
he thought he was."

"I'm sure their bouncers would toss him out, too, if
he tried anything," Fletcher said, and he was smiling
now at the thought.

"You are not a bouncer, though," she said, and she

reached over the barricade, poking him in the chest. "You didn't need to rush to my rescue because I am not some damsel in need of saving."

He tried to fight his widening smile so that he wouldn't infuriate her even more than he already had. But she was so damned beautiful when she was feisty like this. Hell, she was always so damned beautiful. He nodded. "I know. But I didn't want you to get hurt."

He looked at her arm now. The bright lights illuminated the mark on her skin that was still red from how tightly the man had gripped her. And Fletcher wished he'd hit the guy a little harder.

She glanced down at where his gaze was focused and shrugged. "I get bigger bruises than that hauling this equipment around," she said. "That's nothing. And if he'd not let me go, he would have gotten an injury that would have had a terrible effect on his wedding night."

Fletcher chuckled. "Okay. Remind me not to piss you off again."

She nodded. "Oh, I will," she promised.

He chuckled again. "Oh, I have no doubt that you will."

"You're kind of pissing me off right now," she said.

"How's that?"

"You're stalling when we have work to do," she pointed out. "Let's get this equipment out to the SUV."

He tensed. "Are you going to come around to the alley again like when we unloaded it?"

"You're too tired to schlep it out to the parking lot?" she asked with a teasing smile.

"No," he said. "We can do that. But first, I do need to check the alley."

Especially since all his suspects had disappeared a while ago.

What if one of them had attacked someone else while he'd been in the club, drooling over Kiki? He would never forgive himself for getting so distracted.

But he would also never forgive himself if something happened to her. "No. I'll check the alley after I walk you out to your SUV."

She narrowed her eyes and glared at him. "If I thought I needed a guard dog, I'd bring Fancy to work with me."

He chuckled. "Fancy is pretty young to be a guard dog."

"She's feisty."

"Like her owner."

"I'm not her owner," Kiki said with a trace of regret. "Just her foster mom."

"You never get attached to these puppies you foster and want to keep one?" he asked.

She shook her head. "No. I travel too much to have a pet or a relationship."

Was she warning him off? She probably couldn't miss how attracted to her that he was. But it was just attraction. Nothing more.

Attraction and concern.

"We'll carry out some of the lighter things to your vehicle," he said. "Then you can drive it back to the alley and we'll get the heavier stuff."

She sighed but nodded. "Okay."

He was going to make her wait until he checked the alley before she pulled her vehicle into it, though. He didn't want her to find another victim, either with him or without him.

Kiki's irritation with Fletcher slipped away the minute they stepped outside the club. The parking lot wasn't very well lit, like the one in Conners.

And the night was eerily quiet. Not even a cicada sang or a cricket chirped.

Apprehension raced over her like a cold breeze, and she shivered.

"Here," Fletcher said. "Take my shirt." While holding one of her turntables, he managed to pull off his shirt and drape it over her shoulders.

She would have refused, but it was warm, and it smelled like him—like soap and man. "Aren't you worried about someone seeing your holster and gun?" she asked.

"If they're out here in the dark, it might be a good thing if they do," he said.

The Slasher hadn't ever attacked an armed man. So it was definitely a good thing, especially since she suspected Fletcher was going to insist on checking the alley alone once he'd walked her to her vehicle.

Her grandfather would have been charmed by Fletcher's protectiveness and chivalry. Kiki kept trying to tell herself that she was annoyed.

But she might have been just a little bit charmed as well. Not that she was taking it personally. As a lawman, Fletcher had taken that whole oath to protect and serve or serve and protect... Whatever it was.

He was really undercover to protect any more men from being attacked by the Slasher.

Even though she was happy that she wasn't out here alone in this eerie and all-encompassing darkness, she felt compelled to say, "You really don't need to walk me to my vehicle. I'm not in danger from the Slasher."

"We already talked about that," he said. "If he or she feels threatened..."

She snorted. "I'm not carrying the gun, and I have no idea who would do something like that." She certainly hoped she didn't know someone that vicious and evil.

"I'm not just concerned about the Slasher," Fletcher said. "I don't entirely trust that bachelor party groom wouldn't come back after the club closed."

"Then once again, you're probably in more danger than I am," she said. She'd considered that, though, and her pepper spray canister was hooked to one of the belt loops of her red leather shorts. Just in case.

Kiki believed in being better safe than sorry, which was why she wanted to ignore this attraction she felt for Fletcher. But the heat from his shirt, and the scent of him in the fabric, titillated her senses.

"Why'd you park so far out?" Fletcher asked. Clearly, he was more annoyed than titillated.

"I parked out here because I couldn't leave my vehicle in the alley where we unloaded," she reminded him. "And by the time we unloaded it, the lot was already starting to fill up so I had to park out here."

Fletcher groaned.

"We're almost there," she assured him, clicking the key fob so that the lights on her SUV blinked on. "Despite all that coffee I saw you drinking, you're still tired. Not used to staying up so late?"

"It's more these boots you had me buy. As expensive as they were, I expected them to be more comfortable," he grumbled.

"You need to break them in first," she said.

"I thought I was…with the dancing." He did a couple fancy cha-cha steps.

Kiki laughed. She clicked to open the back of her SUV, setting her stuff inside the hatch.

"You've been holding out on me, Colton. You're going to have to salsa with me." She reached out and grasped his hips, trying to move them back as she took a couple of steps toward him. But he didn't move, and suddenly she was flush against his long, hard body. "You're supposed to dance."

"I don't know how to salsa," he said, his voice a little gruff. And even in the dim light from the hatch of her SUV, his eyes glittered as he stared down at her.

The intensity of that stare moved inside her like the music did, making her want him so damn badly. With her heels on, she wasn't that much shorter than he was, so his face wasn't that much above hers. Her gaze moved to his lips, and yearning filled her, making her stretch just a bit until their mouths were so close that there was only a breath between them.

Fletcher groaned.

And Kiki smiled. "Feet still hurting from those new boots?"

"It's not the boots that are bothering me now," he admitted in a husky whisper.

"What's bothering you?" Kiki asked. But as close as she was to him, she could feel his body's reaction to hers.

"You are," he said, and his breath whispered across her mouth.

She parted her lips, breathing him in before releasing a shaky, wistful sigh. "Fletcher…" She couldn't remember the last time she'd been this attracted to someone. And they hadn't even kissed.

She stretched up a bit and brushed her mouth across his. And heat swept through her body.

"This is a bad idea," Fletcher murmured.

"What?" she asked, playing coy.

"I can't afford any distractions right now, not with this investigation, and my cover…" But then he kissed her back, as she'd kissed him, just brushing his mouth across hers before pulling back.

"What's the distraction?" she asked.

"You are," he repeated. "So damn distracting…" And he kissed her again. Deeply. His mouth settling firmly against hers.

She parted her lips and deepened the kiss even more. Their tongues touched, flirted, teased and, again, desire coursed through her like music, making her body want to move with his.

But then that eerie silence broke, something smashing against something, like the sound of glass breaking. They jerked apart, Fletcher reaching for his weapon.

"What? Where…" she murmured.

"Stay here," Fletcher whispered, and he moved back toward the club, disappearing into the darkness.

Had the sound come from the alley? The way it had echoed, it probably had.

Maybe it was just the bartender or someone else who worked at the club dumping something into the trash behind the building. Or…

It was the Slasher attacking another victim, and Fletcher was either going to stop it or put himself in danger as well. Her heart pounded fast and hard with fear.

For him.

Then she heard something closer. And she was scared for herself.

She'd parked so far out that the SUV was near a field. Something moved in the grass, making it rustle softly. It was probably just an animal.

The real threat was in that alley, where Fletcher had rushed off to.

He was the one in danger.

She had no reason to be afraid, except for worrying over him. Maybe she was also afraid over that kiss.

Another sound emanated from the field, something low and forlorn.

Maybe that animal she'd heard was in pain. Hurt.

She took a few tentative steps away from the SUV. Fletcher hadn't meant for her to stay exactly where he'd left her. He just hadn't wanted her to follow him.

She understood that. She had no gun. And she didn't want to be a distraction to him, like he'd already accused her of being. She didn't want him to get hurt because of her.

And she didn't want any other living creature in harm's way either. Peering into the darkness, she walked closer, until she stood just inside the tall weeds of that field. She tilted her head and listened.

Not just for that sound she'd heard but also to the soft rumble of Fletcher's voice. He'd found something in the alley. But he hadn't fired his weapon.

Maybe everything was fine. It had just been what she'd thought: an employee throwing trash into the dumpster. Fletcher was fine.

But then something reached out of the weeds and darkness and grabbed her, and she knew she was the one in danger. As she fumbled for the pepper spray on her belt loop, she opened her mouth and screamed. But if it was the Slasher who'd grabbed her, help would probably come too late to save her.

Chapter 11

One minute Fletcher had been talking to the bartender, Bart Taylor, in the alley where the man had dropped a crate of empty bottles, and the next that scream had rung out.

Kiki's scream.

God, he'd thought she was safe. Safer out there than if she'd followed him into the alley. Fear gripping him, he ran back toward the lot, toward where he'd left her.

But he didn't see her standing near her SUV. The dome lights casting a glow out of the hatch didn't illuminate her. "Kiki?" he called out, his voice cracking a bit with his concern for her.

"Here!" she yelled. "Over here! Call an ambulance!" Her voice was high with fear or adrenaline or both.

"Are you hurt?" he asked, that alarm gripping him still, squeezing his heart.

"Not me. But…there's another victim…"

Fletcher found her standing in a field just beyond her vehicle. She seemed fine, just slightly shaky as she pointed down at the ground.

"I don't want to move him."

Fletcher holstered his weapon and pulled out his cell. The light from the screen illuminated the area and the body lying in the weeds, blood pooling all around it. He was facedown, the back of his head bloodied with maybe a cracked skull.

Fletcher dropped to his knees next to the man, reaching for his wrist to check for a pulse. "Is he dead?"

"No," Kiki said. "He—he grabbed my ankle…"

And Fletcher could see now that the man's arm was outstretched toward Kiki. And there was blood smeared on her skin.

The man's hands and arms were cut. But there was a pulse, albeit faint and slow. Fletcher called in to dispatch, requesting an ambulance and a police response. He glanced around, making sure the bartender wasn't close enough to hear, then he identified himself, gave his badge number and added, "Make sure no one acknowledges me. I'm undercover so question me like any other witness."

But he wasn't like any other witness because he hadn't seen a damn thing. He'd been distracted, just like he'd told Kiki, with her. While he'd kept checking the alley for the Slasher or for another victim, he hadn't thought to check out the parking lot. Hell, he hadn't even noticed anything when he'd walked Kiki to her SUV, and given the blood, the guy had been lying here for a while.

"Should we do something?" Kiki asked. "Roll him over? Make sure he's breathing?"

"With his head wound…" Fletcher was hesitant about moving him. "I don't want to hurt him any worse than he already is."

"But he could be dying."

Fletcher touched the guy's wrist again, and that thready pulse was gone now. His skin even slightly chilled. He hated to move the guy, but in order to administer CPR, the victim had to be on his back.

Fletcher slowly rolled him over, being so careful of his head, and even he gasped while some strangled sound slipped through the hand Kiki had clasped over her mouth.

"Oh, my God…"

There were deep slashes across the guy's face, but despite the wounds, Fletcher recognized him. He was the groom with whom he'd tussled on the dance floor.

"Oh, my God…" Kiki murmured again.

Fletcher didn't know if she recognized him, too, or if she was just horrified by the injuries, the deep lacerations across the guy's face and chest and arms.

He leaned closer to him, listening for breath, watching his damaged chest to see if it was moving, and he heard a soft rattle from it. He was still breathing, but his lungs were filling, probably with blood. "He doesn't need CPR," Fletcher said.

He needed far more help than Fletcher's first aid

training had covered. Sirens whined in the distance, gradually getting louder and louder as the ambulance and police approached. And Fletcher let out a little breath of his own—of relief that help was arriving.

He wasn't sure, though, if they would be able to save the guy either, not with how badly he was wounded. He was by far the most seriously injured of the Slasher's victims.

Just as Fletcher had feared, the level of violence was escalating. And it was only a matter of time before an attack became fatal and claimed a life.

Kiki was shaken. Too shaken to sleep. Too shaken to stay at Grandpa's cottage and not accidentally wake him up while she paced. So she just stopped at his house, picked up Fancy and drove around the lake to the marina where the houseboat was docked.

She wouldn't disturb anyone else here. She'd left a note for Grandpa just in case he had heard her drive up. Knowing how light a sleeper he was, he probably had.

That was why she'd rushed around to get out of the house, with Fancy and a bag of clothes and toiletries, before he came out of his bedroom. She hadn't wanted to talk about what had happened that night.

What she'd found.

The latest victim of the Slasher.

What a maniac. A monster, really, because how could one human being do that to another?

She shuddered despite the fact that she still wore Fletcher's shirt. The cotton was pretty thin, though, and it had lost the warmth of his body that it had when he'd first given it to her.

He'd lost his warmth, too, when the ambulance and the police had arrived. He'd been all business, talking to everyone else almost furtively, probably because he hadn't wanted to blow his cover.

And another officer or detective had questioned her. Kiki had been so shocked by what she'd found, by that hand reaching out of the darkness and the weeds to grasp her ankle.

The scream had been instinctive, but her throat burned a little from how loudly she'd uttered it. And she trembled again from the terror she'd felt in that moment.

Fancy whimpered. Either the puppy had picked up on Kiki's fear, or she was nervous walking down the dock toward the houseboat.

Water lapped against the boats they passed and against the posts of the dock, swirling around them in the faint light of the sliver of the moon overhead.

Where had that moon been earlier?

She could have used that in the parking lot. Then maybe she would have found him sooner.

The way the EMTs had looked—from how furiously they'd been working to the way they'd sped away, lights flashing and siren ringing out loudly…

It hadn't looked good.

She didn't know if he was going to make it. And she felt a pang of guilt for how she'd felt about the man earlier that evening, when he'd grabbed her arm.

It had been him, hadn't it?

Another groom-to-be celebrating his bachelor party

like the last victim of the Slasher. What the hell did that person have against men like that?

Sure, this guy, whoever he was, had been a jerk. But the other man…

The victim she'd visited in the hospital hadn't seemed arrogant like that one. He'd even managed, despite his injuries, to laugh with her.

She wondered if tonight's victim would ever be able to laugh again. She wondered if she would, after finding him.

No wonder that Fletcher always seemed so intense. This was his life, the career he'd chosen for himself. To investigate crimes like the one that Kiki had literally stumbled across tonight.

The body.

No. The person. He had to live.

"Oh, Fancy…" Kiki murmured, her heart heavy with dread. With regret.

Maybe if she and Fletcher had done things differently…

Maybe if the man hadn't been evicted from the club…

Maybe he wouldn't have been hurt so badly.

Maybe he would be…

He had to be fine.

She wasn't sure that she would be again, after what she'd seen. She needed a beer and some soft music. Grandpa kept beer in the fridge in the galley on the boat. And she always had music with her. Either on her phone, or just inside her.

Maybe if she sang to herself…

People had said she was singing when she'd been found, in the wreckage of the crash that had killed her parents.

The wreckage she had escaped without a scratch on her. She didn't remember any of that. Maybe wiping the memories from her mind had been her childlike way of dealing with that horrific tragedy.

But she wasn't a child anymore. And she doubted she would be able to forget anything about tonight. About finding that man.

Or about that kiss she'd shared with Fletcher. If not for whatever had happened in the alley, maybe they would have...

No. Not in a parking lot. She wasn't some wild teenager. She never had been. She'd been tempted in that moment to act like a hormonal teen, though, to give in to her desire for Fletcher.

Thinking about that kiss should have been better than thinking about what had happened after it, but her pulse quickened even more. And the adrenaline was rushing through her again.

That kiss had been dangerous to her.

But why?

Fletcher had said he wasn't ever getting married, that he didn't have time for relationships either. And she certainly understood why. His work was definitely more important. Catching the Slasher was absolutely more important.

That was why, after answering the officer's questions, she'd left. The club had been pretty much sealed off, probably as a crime scene, so she trusted that her equipment would be safe there overnight.

She had another gig there this weekend, if the club was allowed to reopen, so it made sense to leave it there anyway. It was just so expensive, though, that she usually preferred to keep it with her.

But after what had happened to that man, she'd realized how inconsequential material things were. People mattered more. Maybe she should have stayed at Grandpa's.

But he was safe. Nothing was going to happen to him.

He was long past the age when he used to come to the clubs to watch her. She didn't have to worry about the Slasher attacking him.

But she still worried about him.

He'd always been there for her. She couldn't imagine a world without him in it.

Fancy whimpered again, reminding Kiki that she'd just stopped on the dock. She was near the houseboat, but her thoughts had been weighing so heavily on her that it seemed hard to step across the side and onto the boat deck. As if she might slip and fall between the boat and the dock.

Fancy probably feared that, too, because the puppy whimpered again.

"It's okay," Kiki assured her, and she bent over to scoop the puppy up in her arms. She held her close for a moment, burying her face in the dog's soft fur. Instead of reassuring the puppy, she was looking for comfort.

Maybe she should have woken up Grandpa. He had

always been so good at comforting her. At making her feel better about everything.

But he was getting older, and she didn't want to burden him with things like this, things that would make him worry more about her than he already did.

And he already worried too much.

She understood, though, because she worried about him, too. She didn't want to lose him like they'd already lost her mother and father. She didn't want to lose anyone else she loved. Another reason she needed to make sure this attraction she felt for Fletcher didn't go any deeper, didn't become real feelings.

After tonight, she realized all too well just how dangerous his job was. That could have been him bleeding out in the blood-soaked, overgrown field.

She shuddered. And Fancy bristled in her arms. "Sorry," she murmured to the puppy. She was definitely not making the little dog less nervous.

"Here," she said. And she passed the dog over the side of the boat before stepping onto the deck herself. The boat rocked a bit on the softly lapping water.

Then Fancy headed toward the door to the cabin. The open door.

It should have been locked. Kiki had certainly locked it the last time she'd been here. What about Grandpa? Had he forgotten?

He certainly believed Owl Creek was safer than anywhere else, which was why he preferred it when she was home. He had no idea how dangerous this place could be.

But after tonight, Kiki knew.

And she wondered if that danger had found her here.

Chapter 12

"Where the hell is she?" Fletcher asked.

But the night had no answer for him as he stood outside Jim's cottage. Her SUV wasn't parked in the driveway like it should have been, like he'd hoped it would be.

Sometime after she'd been questioned, she'd slipped away from the club. From the crime scene.

She'd even left her equipment behind, which had alarmed him. Why wouldn't she have waited for his help to load it up? Why would she have taken off without it?

While her equipment had been there, his duffel bag had gone missing. With that glass inside.

The bartender had stayed to answer questions, though, as had a couple of the waitresses, bouncers and dishwashers. They had all made certain to share that the last time they'd seen the victim had been when he'd been fighting with Fletcher over Kiki.

Was that why she'd taken off?

Did she suspect him of being involved like the club employees had?

No. The officer who'd questioned her had assured Fletcher that she'd alibied him. Even if the officer hadn't known that he was a detective, the young woman would have ruled him out as a suspect then.

Not that she was running the investigation. He was.

He told himself that was why he needed to find Kiki. But even he knew he was lying about that. He needed to find Kiki to make sure that she was all right. That she wasn't too upset about finding the latest victim of the Slasher and that the Slasher hadn't followed her from the crime scene.

Could they have been worried that she'd seen something?

Was that why they'd attacked the latest victim so far from the alley? So it would be harder for anyone to see the attack? Or to find the body?

This assault had been far more vicious than the others. And the blow to the head…

That was new. None of the other victims had had a wound like that, none had been hit over the head so hard that it had rendered them unconscious.

The wounded man hadn't regained consciousness after the paramedics had arrived either. Would he? On his way to Kiki's house, Fletcher had called the hospital in Conners where the man had been taken since there was only an express medical clinic in Owl Creek.

After identifying himself, Fletcher had asked for an update on the victim's condition.

From the wallet found on him, with all his money and credit cards in it, Fletcher knew the guy's name was Gregory Stehouwer. Stehouwer was in a coma. His head injury had been that severe, and they weren't sure he would wake up. Maybe he'd seen the Slasher. Could that be why he'd been hit so hard in the head? Maybe the Slasher had tried to kill him so that this victim wouldn't be able to identify them.

From the extent of that blow, Fletcher was beginning to lean toward a male assailant or a very strong female. The only thing Fletcher knew for certain about the Slasher was how dangerous they were.

So dangerous that he'd needed to make sure that Kiki had gotten safely home. But she wasn't home. Where the hell was she? And had she gone there on her own or had someone forced her to go where they'd wanted her to?

Or was he just overreacting because he'd been so damn shaken when she'd screamed?

He sighed, uncertain of whether or not he should knock. If he woke up Jim and alarmed him and she was fine, she would be furious. But if something had happened to her and he'd done nothing to find her...

"Who's out there?" a gruff voice called from the darkness within the house.

"Mr. Shelton?" he called back. "It's Fletcher Colton, sir."

A bright light flashed on, momentarily blinding him. He squinted and turned slightly away from the porch light.

"It is you," Jim Shelton said as he pulled open the interior door and peered at Fletcher through the screen. "Has something happened? What are you doing here?"

Fletcher's tongue stuck to the roof of his mouth for a moment as he considered his answer. Then he cleared his throat and said, "I saw Kiki at the club earlier tonight, and I had to follow up about something she saw."

Shelton released a heavy sigh. "Something happen again like that one in Conners and the other in Salt Lake City?"

Those weren't the only places where the Slasher had attacked, but those were the most recent. Fletcher gave a noncommittal shrug. "I don't know for certain, sir." And as he said it, he realized that it was true.

The whole MO of this felt so different than the other attacks and not just because of how severely the victim had been injured, but because he'd been so far from the club. The other victims had been left in the alley, where someone would almost certainly find him when they were cleaning up after the club closed.

This victim had been left out in a field beyond the parking lot, as if nobody had wanted him to be found. Or, at least, maybe not with enough time to save him.

"And you think Kiki will know what happened?" Shelton asked, and he stared intently through that screen.

Fletcher shrugged. "I don't know." Then, because he was being honest, he added, "Probably not."

Instead of being concerned, the older man chuckled. "Thought there was something-something between the two of you even at your daddy's funeral. Sorry about that, son. I really thought that Robert was too tough to die, at least so damn young."

To a man in his late seventies or early eighties, fifty-nine was young. Hell, to Fletcher, fifty-nine was young no matter how hard his dad had lived those years. Working too much, drinking, smoking and eating too much.

"How's your mama doing?" Shelton asked.

While not everybody had been a fan of his dad's, they all loved his mom. "She's doing well, sir," Fletcher replied. "More worried about the rest of us than herself."

"Sounds like your mama," Shelton said with a smile. "My Kiki is a lot like her—always worrying about me when she should be worrying about herself."

Fletcher was worried enough about her right now for the both of them. But he didn't want to concern her grandfather too much. At least not until he knew where and how she was.

"Have any idea where she might be, sir?" he asked.

Shelton chuckled. "Of course. She left a note when she picked up the puppy."

Fletcher should have realized that he hadn't heard the little shepherd yet. And if it had been here, the puppy probably would have been jumping on him. "Where did she go, sir?" he asked.

"The houseboat."

Blackbird Lake was so big that there were a few marinas on it as well as many, many private docks. Obviously, the houseboat wasn't docked at the cottage, or Kiki's vehicle would have been parked in the driveway where Fletcher had been hoping to find it.

"Where is that, sir?"

The older man pushed open the screen door and stepped onto the porch with Fletcher. "I'm not sure I should tell you since she didn't leave you a note."

Fletcher smiled. "I think she figured I was busy, so she didn't bother saying good-bye when she left." At least he hoped that was reason she had.

"And you really want to say good-bye to her?" Shelton pushed. The older man was shrewd. He obviously knew Fletcher was interested in his granddaughter.

But Fletcher didn't want him to know how worried about her he was. "I need to ask her a few questions, too."

Like if she regretted kissing him now. Or if she regretted it having to stop, like he did.

Most of all, he just wanted to make sure that she was safe.

"What the hell happened tonight?" Shelton asked, his voice sharper now as if he was irritated. "You know I'll hear about it."

Fletcher had made certain that there had been no reporters at the club tonight, and the ones who'd shown up in Conners had been denied a story. Nobody had answered any of their questions, and he'd also taken steps to protect the investigation from the Freedom of Information Act for now. Since it was an ongoing investigation, no reports could be shared with the public. He wanted to starve the Slasher of the very thing he or she seemed to crave most: fame.

But maybe that was why the Slasher had struck again so close to the last attack. Maybe he or she was chasing headlines, trying to get into the news again. Trying to get attention.

And if so, maybe Fletcher was to blame for that man's attack tonight. Not directly, like the bartender and other club staff had seemed to imply, but indirectly.

And when he'd thrown the man out of the club, he'd just about delivered him to the Slasher. But the guy hadn't left alone. Some of his entourage had left with him. Had he returned on his own?

For Kiki? Maybe that was why he'd been attacked near her vehicle.

"I really can't say, sir," Fletcher said. "You know how quickly gossip spreads in Owl Creek."

"But would it be gossip?" Shelton asked.

Fletcher sighed. "Not exactly gossip…but not exactly fact either. Until an investigation is complete, it's all pretty much just speculation."

Fletcher had been doing a lot of that because he'd had no real leads to the Slasher until now. Now he had many leads to follow. The bartender. The distraught father.

And Kiki's missing assistant.

He just hoped none of them had followed Kiki from the club and then to wherever this houseboat was.

"You're about as slippery as that minister from that strange, fairy-tale church."

"Fairy-tale church?"

"You know. The Ever After Church."

Fletcher tensed. That was the church that the guy who'd gone after Ruby had been obsessed with, so much so that he'd been trying to get Crosswinds for them. Supposedly unbeknownst to the pastor, though.

Or was it?

"Markus Acker?" Fletcher asked.

"What?"

"The minister you're talking about," Fletcher prodded him.

"Yeah, that's probably it," the older man said with a shrug. "I've only seen him a couple of times, usually running around the countryside." Then Jim Shelton yawned.

Fletcher had been so tired himself earlier, but once he'd kissed Kiki…

All hell had broken loose in more ways than one. "Sir," he prodded the man. "I really need to talk to your granddaughter."

Shelton sniffed as if he was smelling a load of bullshit. And he kind of was.

Fletcher wasn't being entirely honest with him. And even the old man must have realized that Fletcher wanted to do more than talk to her. What had he called it? The something-something between them?

Fletcher grinned.

And the old man chuckled and shook his head. "You can go see her." He gave him the name of the marina and the slip number. "But don't say I didn't warn you."

"Warn me? About what?"

"Kiki's not settling down anytime soon," Shelton said. "She only comes here as much as she does out of obligation for me."

"Love," Fletcher corrected him.

And Shelton grinned. "Yeah, she's a sweetheart. But she's also as stubborn as…" His grin widened. "As her grandfather. Nobody's going to tie that girl down or tell her what to do."

"I don't want to tie her down," Fletcher assured him. But now...

He shook his head to clear those kinds of *something-something* thoughts from it.

He just wanted to make sure that she was all right.

"I know," Shelton said with another yawn. "You want to *talk* to her."

Fletcher nodded. "Thanks for telling me where she is." And he hoped like hell that the old man was right that she was at the houseboat.

Safe.

But a sudden chill rushed over him, and his fear returned. And he felt like he had when he'd heard her scream.

Like she was in danger.

Kiki may have stood there for seconds, frozen on the deck as she stared at the open door. But it wasn't just open. The glass in the door had been broken; shards of it littered the deck, sparkling in the faint glow of that crescent moon.

Grandpa hadn't forgotten to lock the houseboat. Neither had Kiki.

Someone had broken in. Were they still there?

She'd stood there, frozen, wondering what to do. Call the cops? Grab her pepper spray? But Fancy hadn't stayed beside her. Instead she'd walked over that glass and into the cabin area of the houseboat.

Now she barked and then yipped, like she'd been

hurt. Thinking of that man, how badly he'd been injured, Kiki charged forward, her pepper spray clasped tightly in her hand. She wasn't even scared. She was furious.

"Don't hurt her!" she yelled. "Don't you dare hurt her!" With her free hand, she fumbled for the switch inside the galley kitchen. Light flickered on over her head and spilled into the living area of the boat and onto the man who lay on the couch, the dog nipping at his worn jeans. "Troy!"

"I'm not hurting her," he said, as he pushed the dog back.

The puppy nipped at his hand.

"Fancy!" she called. The dog turned toward her, and she made the gesture of her hand at her side, palm up, and then bent it toward her opposite shoulder. The shoulder of her hand that still held the pepper spray. "Come."

The dog glanced back at Troy, as if still uncertain of him, before finally obeying Kiki's command. She planted her bristling little puppy body, her hair raised, between Kiki and Troy. Her protectiveness was as instinctual as Sebastian considered her "scent" skills. Maybe Fletcher's need to protect was just as instinctual.

If only he could have protected her from what she'd seen…

Did she need protection now? From Troy?

"What the hell are you doing here?" she asked. "The police are looking for you."

"I know," he said. "That's why I'm here. You showed me this place when I first got to Owl Creek."

On the way to show him the campground where he'd rented a space, she'd stopped off at the marina to check on the boat. He'd been nervous around the water, though, as nervous as he'd been around the club.

She'd thought he'd just been on edge after what he'd seen in Salt Lake City. After finding that victim...

Was Fletcher right? Was that too much of a coincidence?

But then she'd been working the club in Conners and then tonight...

She resisted the urge to shudder over the memory of what she'd found, of how that hand had wrapped around her ankle and she'd thought it was the Slasher that grabbed her, not the Slasher's latest victim.

"I didn't intend for you to use this boat, especially not to hide out from the authorities," she said.

"I'm not... I can't..." he stammered.

"They just want to talk to you about what happened at that club in Conners last weekend," she said. Had he been here all week?

He swung his legs down from the couch and sat up.

She tensed, worried that he was going to jump up, that he was going to come at her since she was between him and the door. The door that he'd broken to get inside.

Could she trust him? She knew now how very little he'd told her about himself.

But instead of getting up, he leaned forward and put his head in his hands. "That's so messed up, Kiki."

"Yes, it is," she agreed.

"I'm sorry I didn't get there in time to help you tonight," he said.

She tensed. "You were at the club tonight?"

"Yeah. I showed up late, though, and you had someone else there," he said, with a hurt tone, almost as if she'd betrayed him. "Who is he?"

The lawman who considered him the prime suspect in his Slasher case.

"An old friend," she said. "I've known him for years." That was true. But she'd left out important details, just like Troy had about himself. Troy had left out that he was a criminal. She'd left out that Fletcher was a cop. "I thought you were a friend, too, Troy, but then I realized how little I know about you."

He looked up at her then. "You know me, Kiki. We've known each other for years."

"Yes," she said. "But how is it possible that I didn't even know your last name?"

"You never asked."

She could kick herself now for not vetting her assistant more thoroughly. That another DJ had been using him for years wasn't an excuse. She realized that now. "And I didn't know about your criminal record either."

"The cops told you about that?" he asked, and he sucked in a breath.

Was he worried about her knowing? Or that the police knew? Probably the police, since he was hiding from them. What would he do to stay hidden?

She tightened her grasp on her pepper spray. She didn't want to use it, but she would if she felt threatened. "Yes, they were concerned with you taking off after that man was wounded at the club. You need to talk to them."

"I didn't see anything," Troy said, his voice rising with irritation. "I've got nothing to tell them!"

Fancy barked.

"Heel," Kiki told the puppy. She didn't want Troy doing to Fancy whatever he'd done that had made the dog yelp before Kiki had followed her into the houseboat cabin. "They still need to speak to you, Troy. To rule you out—"

"I'm a suspect?" he interjected and jumped up then.

And Fancy jumped too, her body bristling as she growled low in her throat. The puppy obviously didn't trust Troy any more than Fletcher did, and probably any more than Kiki should.

She needed to call the police.

Or Fletcher.

Troy raised his foot, as if to kick Fancy who'd jumped toward him.

"No!" Kiki screamed. "Don't hurt—"

Pounding cut off her protest. The sound of running footsteps against the dock. She whirled around and Troy shoved past her, knocking her back against the kitchen cabinets. Then his footsteps echoed that other pounding. And then a splash.

And the boat rocked, hitting against the dock.

Somebody had gone into the lake.

Troy?

Or whoever had been running down the dock?

To rescue her?

Or...

Chapter 13

Kiki's scream affected Fletcher the way it had at the club. His heart pounded with fear for her, for her safety. For her life.

She'd only let out the first note, and he'd started running down the dock, toward the slip number where her grandfather had said he would find the boat.

She had to be on it. Probably inside, because her scream had been a bit muffled. He'd heard the "Don't hurt—" and panicked. He'd drawn his weapon and started running.

He didn't need to check the slip numbers to find her boat because a man leaped off it, onto the dock, and started running toward the end of it. Toward the water.

In the moonlight, Fletcher could see the guy's long, straggly hair and the tattoos on his arms. Was this Troy?

The same Troy others had seen at the club tonight? And then he'd come back here?

Had he been hiding? Or had he suspected that Kiki would come out to the boat and he'd been lying in wait for her? She had to be okay. Through the glass window of the cabin, Fletcher could see her standing.

She didn't look to be injured.

And Fletcher couldn't let Troy escape from him again. So he chased after him. And when Troy jumped off the end of the dock into the water, Fletcher holstered his weapon and followed him into the lake.

Despite it being mid-June, the water was surprisingly cold. And it sucked at Fletcher's clothes and boots.

Those already heavy boots got heavier as the leather sopped up the water. And they began to drag him down, like cement blocks tied to his feet. He kicked and chopped at the water with his arms, trying to fight his way back to the surface as the breath he'd held burned in his lungs.

He had to get out of the lake now, or he might not be able to. He couldn't see anything in the water. Troy might have gotten out. Or Fletcher might have gone so deep that he couldn't see even the moonlight on the surface anymore.

He kicked harder, using his strength. Suddenly light shone on him, and he realized he was at the surface again. But the boots kept pulling at him, dragging him down. He reached out for the dock, grabbing one of the wood posts.

The light shining on him was from a cell phone held

in Kiki's hand. "Are you all right?" she asked. "Do I need to call 9-1-1?"

He panted for air, dragging in deep gulps of it while hanging on to that post. He had to pull himself up and out before his grasp on that post slipped. "I'll be fine…" he said between pants.

The light dimmed. And then Kiki reached down to grab his arms and try to pull him up. He worked with her until finally he lay on the dock, water dripping from his saturated clothes.

"Are you all right?" she asked again as she knelt beside him, leaning over him. She was so beautiful and held so much concern in her dark eyes.

And he remembered that kiss in the parking lot before everything had gone to hell.

"Want to give me mouth to mouth?" he asked, unable to resist teasing her.

She chuckled and leaned back. "I guess you are all right then."

He nodded then tensed. "Troy? Where is he?"

"He got out of the water before you did," she said, her breath hitching a little.

"Did he hurt you?" he asked, reaching up to grasp her arms.

She flinched and shook her head.

"But you're hurt."

"That's from that other guy on the dance floor."

He had hurt her, but despite that, he hadn't deserved what had happened to him.

"Did he make it?" she asked, her voice cracking slightly now.

"The last update I got, he was alive, but in a coma," Fletcher shared. And he'd just let one of the suspects in his attack get away. He used his elbows to push himself up so that he was sitting. "Where did Troy go?"

She shrugged. "He got out of the lake farther down the shore." She pointed in the distance. "And ran off into the woods."

Fletcher struggled to roll over onto his knees and then push himself up to his feet. But his legs were weak from all the kicking he'd had to do to keep from getting sucked to the bottom of the lake, and they nearly folded beneath him.

Kiki caught him around the waist. "You're not going to catch him even if you could run."

He could barely take a step; his boots were so heavy with water that it was hard to lift his foot. "These damn boots," he grumbled.

"Yeah, it's the boots," Kiki said. "Grandpa leaves some clothes on the boat. Let's get you something dry."

"But Troy…" He'd been so damn close to catching him. To maybe catching the Slasher. He had to stop that maniac, had to make sure that he didn't hurt anyone else.

"He's gone," she repeated. "And he got a hell of a head start on you. You're not going to find him."

He pulled his cell from his pocket, and water streamed out of the case. He cursed.

"Do you want to call 9-1-1?" she asked. "I have my phone."

Fletcher shook his head and spattered water around the dock and across her face.

"You're like a dog," she remarked.

And he glanced around. "Your grandpa said you had Fancy. Did something happen to her?" He hated to think of the sweet little pup being injured.

"I locked her in the bathroom on the boat," she said. "I didn't want her getting in the water. Or Troy hurting her."

"Troy hurt her?" he asked. A man who could hurt an animal could easily hurt people, too.

Her teeth lightly nipped her bottom lip and she shrugged. "I don't know. She got onto the houseboat before I did, and she made a yipping noise. She seems fine though."

"Want me to call Ruby?" he asked. "Have her check Fancy out?"

"No," she said. "Ruby's pregnant. She needs her rest, especially after what she went through and then losing your dad so soon after that. We can't wake her up."

Fletcher's heart warmed with a flood of appreciation for this woman. "You're a good friend to her." So good that he shouldn't have involved Kiki in his undercover operation. He'd put her in danger.

And Ruby would probably never forgive him if something happened to her friend because of him.

"This was a bad idea," he murmured.

"What?"

He glanced around, wondering who else he and Troy might have awakened when they'd run down the dock. There were quite a few other boats in the marina. And maybe Troy wasn't as far away as Kiki thought he was.

Maybe he had circled around and come back. Maybe he was out there somewhere, listening.

Waiting.

Fletcher couldn't talk to her here. And he had to make sure that his weapon worked after jumping in the lake with it, in case Troy came back.

"Where's that boat?" he asked. And he pulled his T-shirt away from his body.

"I'm sorry," she said. "You must be getting cold." But she was the one that shivered as a breeze blew across the lake, making all the boats rock. "It's this way."

Her arm was still around his waist, as if she thought he needed help walking. While his boots were still so heavy, his strength had returned along with his usual reaction to her nearness: attraction. So he pulled away from her.

She still wore his shirt—the one he'd given her at the club. And it was wet now, her red leather vest showing through it.

"You're probably cold," he remarked. But he sure wasn't, not when just looking at her had heat flashing through him. Along with that damn desire he had no business feeling, not in the middle of a dangerous investigation. Not when his cover was putting her in danger.

"I'm fine," she said as she led the way down the long dock. She stopped outside a houseboat. Whimpering emanated from somewhere inside it.

"Poor Fancy," he said. "Are you sure she's all right?" He jumped over to the boat deck. And glass crunched beneath his wet boots. "He broke in here."

"Yes."

"To do what?" he asked. "Wait for you?"

"I think he was just hiding out," Kiki said. "But he admitted to being at the club earlier."

Fletcher cursed. Had he been that close to the Slasher just to lose him in the water?

Fancy must have heard Fletcher's voice because her whimpering became yips again. But not yips of pain. Yips of excitement.

The puppy had fallen hard for Fletcher.

Kiki had to make sure the dog was the only one who fell for him. Not her.

She couldn't stop shaking, but it wasn't with cold. She'd been so scared when he hadn't surfaced from the water. She'd known it was him when she'd heard that splash. Him who'd come clomping so loudly down the dock in the boots that had probably nearly killed him.

But he was strong. He'd fought his way to the surface again. And now he rushed inside the houseboat.

Fancy's yips got louder when he opened the bathroom door. And when Kiki joined them inside, she found him running his hands over the little dog as if checking her for injuries like his sister, the vet, would have.

His genuine concern for the puppy got under Kiki's skin in the best possible way. As if he wasn't hard enough to resist with the way his wet clothes had molded against his muscular body.

With the way his slick hair highlighted all those chiseled features of his handsome face...

"I think she's okay," he said. "She's not flinching or pulling away from me."

That was because the dog was smart. She liked those big hands of his moving over her little furry body. And suddenly Kiki was very jealous of the puppy. She wanted those big hands of his moving over her body. But she wanted to be naked. And she wanted him naked, too.

"I'm glad she's okay," Kiki said.

"That's why you screamed," Fletcher said. "Because you were worried he was going to hurt her?"

She nodded. "But I don't want to talk about Troy right now," she said. She didn't want to talk at all. "You need to get out of those wet clothes."

Maybe he'd picked up on the huskiness in her voice as the desire she felt for him grew, because he tensed and met her gaze. His green eyes darkened as his pupils dilated. "Kiki…" he murmured, and his voice was even raspier than hers.

And Fancy wriggled down from him to go over to the couch and sniff at it before dropping down on it, her head on her paws as if exhausted.

Maybe she was.

Kiki should have been, too, but adrenaline still coursed through her body, making her tremble. "Is this what you think is a bad idea?" she asked, referring to that comment he'd made on the dock but hadn't expounded on.

He clenched his jaw so tightly that a muscle twitched in his cheek. Then he sighed. "I shouldn't have involved you in this investigation. I shouldn't have put you in danger."

"You didn't," she said.

"But Troy—"

"Is my assistant," she reminded him. "I know you think he's the Slasher, too, but I can't imagine…" She shook her head. "I don't want to talk about Troy. And everything else that happened would have happened whether you were there or not. You didn't put me in danger."

She had.

And she was probably the most at risk right now. But she didn't care. She stepped closer to him and told him, "Take off your clothes."

He sucked in a breath and murmured her name again almost as if he was warning her. He didn't have to say anything else.

"I know," she said. "This is a bad idea. But nobody needs to know about this but us."

"You're already distracting me," he said. "If we—"

She shrugged off the shirt she wore over her vest. His shirt which was wet from where she'd touched him. Then she reached for the zipper at the front of her vest. "Maybe if we do this, we'll be less distracted," she suggested.

He chuckled. "Somehow I don't think it'll work like that." But he leaned down to take off his boots. His holster followed. He took a few minutes to take his weapon apart, probably to let it dry out.

Before he could do anything else, Kiki took his hand in hers and tugged him toward her bedroom. She had her own on the boat just like her grandpa had his, although he rarely stayed there now. After pushing open the pocket door, she stepped into the room, which was so small that there wasn't much floor space around the queen-size bed. So she climbed onto it and reached again for the zipper on her vest, pulling it down so that the red leather fell away from her.

Fletcher groaned as if he was in pain.

"Did you get hurt when you jumped in the lake?" she asked, concerned now that she hadn't called 9-1-1.

He shook his head. "No. You're the one killing me. You're so damn beautiful." He leaned over then and pressed his mouth against hers, kissing her deeply, sliding his tongue between her open lips.

She groaned now. No. She moaned. Then she pulled back. "You need to take off your wet clothes," she reminded him. And she reached for the button on his jeans.

He shoved what looked like the ammo clip from his gun into his pocket. Then he pulled his wet T-shirt over his head as she lowered his zipper.

His breath hissed out as her fingers brushed over his boxers, over his straining erection. As she pushed his jeans down over his lean hips, he slid her open vest from her shoulders, freeing her breasts.

And his breath hissed out again. "You are so beautiful." He cupped her breasts in his hands, running his thumbs over her skin and then over her nipples.

She moaned again as pleasure coursed through her. Her breasts had always been sensitive, but never more so than now. In this moment.

He lowered his head then and closed his mouth around one breast and stroked his tongue across her tight nipple.

"Fletcher," she whispered. She wanted him so badly.

Then he was undoing the button and lowering her

zipper and pulling off her shorts and underwear. "Are you sure?" he asked, his voice gruff with the desire burning in his eyes.

Like it burned inside her.

She eagerly nodded. "Very sure and very impatient." She wanted to go fast and furiously, joining their bodies.

But he took his time. As he turned his attention to her other breast with his mouth, his hands moved over her body. He caressed her skin, traced her curves and then he touched her core.

And she whimpered like Fancy had.

And Fancy yipped with concern.

Fletcher got up and closed the door. Then he was back between her legs. And he made love to her with his mouth and his tongue, driving her out of her mind until pleasure coursed through her with an orgasm that left her quivering.

But it wasn't enough. She wanted more. So she pushed him back onto the bed and pulled off his boxers. Then she lowered her mouth to his shaft. She closed her lips around him, and he tensed. Then he was gently pushing her shoulders back.

"No. I want to be inside you," he said, his voice hoarse. "I need to be inside you." Then he cursed. "But I don't have any—"

She fumbled inside a small cupboard next to the bed, feeling around until she found a packet. She tore it open with her teeth and rolled the condom over him. He was so big. So hard.

She straddled him, easing him inside her until he

filled her. The sensation had her muscles tensing again, pressure building inside her. She leaned down, her breasts rubbing against his chest. The hair tickled her skin, teased her nipples. She moaned and moved.

And he grasped her hips and thrust up, driving deeper. Driving her out of her mind.

It was like they were dancing to the same music, the same beat inside them, their hearts pounding together. They moved in unison.

Then his hands moved from her hips to her breasts, and he stroked her nipples with his thumbs.

She came again, intensely, and a cry of pleasure slipped through her lips. Then he tensed beneath her and began to pulsate inside her as he found his release.

His pleasure.

Her name slipped through his gritted teeth.

She couldn't remember the last time she'd ever been so in sync with a lover. Maybe never.

Fletcher rolled her onto her back and kissed her, brushing his mouth lightly across hers, as he drew out of her body. Then he opened the pocket door and disappeared for a while.

She had just begun to wonder if he'd left when he came back, smelling like soap and midnight rain and sex. And she welcomed him back into her bed, into her arms.

They made love again, slowly, savoring every second. And after another soul-shattering orgasm, she fell asleep. She didn't know how long she'd been out when she felt Fletcher jump next to her.

He must have fallen asleep, too, only to jerk awake.

Then she heard it, the noise he must have heard. The sound of Fancy's low growl. Was she warning them of an intruder?

Had someone broken into the houseboat once again?

Chapter 14

Tension gripped Fletcher as he silently cursed himself. How the hell had he fallen asleep?

He knew how, though. He'd been completely satiated and exhausted and comfortable. And he hadn't wanted his time with Kiki to end.

But no matter what she'd said, he'd put her in danger once again. The way Fancy growled outside the bedroom door indicated that there was some kind of threat out there.

Had Troy come back? Was he going to finish whatever he'd intended to do to Kiki?

Because Fletcher wasn't as convinced as she was that the man had just been hiding out on the houseboat. What if he'd been waiting for her to come back here?

What had he intended to do to her?

And if he was the Slasher, and armed with that dangerously sharp weapon that had already wounded so many others, how the hell was Fletcher going to defend her and himself?

He'd left his gun in pieces, drying out on the counter in the main cabin area. The magazine of ammo was in his jeans. Jeans he quickly stepped into and pulled up.

But before he could reach for the door, Kiki grabbed his arm as if trying to hold him back. "What is it?" she whispered, her voice a little shaky. She was as wide awake as he was now.

"I don't know," he whispered back. But he was going to damn well find out.

"Take my pepper spray," she said, pressing a small canister in his hand.

He closed his hand around it. While it wasn't his gun, it was better than nothing. If the Slasher couldn't see, maybe he or she wouldn't be able to slice Fletcher up like they had their other victims.

He drew in a breath and then opened the pocket door. Morning had come, and sunshine poured through the windows in the houseboat cabin. In the middle of the living room area, Fancy did battle, growling and gnawing on one of the Fletcher's new boots.

Fletcher released the breath he'd been holding and chuckled.

Kiki leaned around him and peered out. Then she pushed past him and ran over to the puppy. Fortunately, for Fletcher's sake, she'd pulled on a terry cloth robe. "Drop it," she commanded the dog as she pointed at the floor.

The puppy whined and wagged her tail as she kept the boot tightly clamped in her mouth.

"I understand why she'd want to destroy those things," Fletcher said. "I'm not too fond of them myself."

"Drop it," Kiki repeated, pointing at the floor again.

Fancy whined one more time, as if pleading with Kiki before she finally dropped the mangled heap of damp leather.

"Impressive," Fletcher said. "You really know a lot about dog training."

Kiki shrugged. "I wanted to learn so that we can start getting her familiar with commands right away."

"Show me," he said. He wasn't really interested. He just didn't want to leave her. Not yet. Maybe not ever.

He pushed the thought aside and focused on the commands that she showed him.

"She doesn't know all of them yet," Kiki said. "We introduce them one at a time." She showed him Sit, which was holding out her hand in front of her, with her palm facing up, then raising it toward her shoulder. "Wait and Stay are almost the same." She held her hand out in front of her, her palm facing Fancy. "And probably the most important to keep her out of trouble."

She showed him a couple more. Lie Down and Up.

"She knows quite a few."

"She's a smart dog," Kiki said.

"And you're a good trainer. Maybe you've missed your calling."

"Music is my calling," she insisted. "I love it."

"I can tell that, too," he said.

"Do you love being a detective?" she asked.

He nodded. "It can be frustrating at times." Like now, trying to catch the Slasher.

"And dangerous," she added.

He shrugged. "Life is full of dangers."

And he'd faced one of the most perilous situations last night. Not when he'd jumped in the lake and nearly drowned. But when he'd drowned in her last night, in the emotions overwhelming him.

He wanted to be with her again. But he'd already dropped the ball on this investigation too many times. "I have to go," he said. The clock on the wall alarmed him. "I didn't realize it was so late already."

Her bedroom had been dark and so very comfortable with her soft bed and her softer body curled up in his arms.

"You were up late," she reminded him.

He wasn't sure if she was talking about the club or about what they'd done in the bed. But he nodded. "I need to go, to check on the victim from last night."

She tensed and nodded. "Yes, let me know how he's doing."

They both hesitated, staring at each other. He didn't want to leave her. He found an excuse for that. "You shouldn't stay here by yourself. Just in case Troy comes back."

"After you chased him off the dock, I doubt he's going to come back," she said. "But I should go back to Grandpa's, make sure he knows I'm okay, just in case he heard anything about last night. Did you tell him about it?"

He shook his head. "No. I didn't want to worry him."

"He already worries too much about me," Kiki said.

"He's going to hear about it," Fletcher said. "I'm trying to keep it all out of the press, but people are going to talk to the media eventually or post something somewhere."

"Like they did after the attack in Salt Lake City," she said. "I saw the reports about it right away."

"These last two attacks weren't discovered until after closing," Fletcher said. "That's why they were easier to keep quiet. And club employees don't want to talk about them and risk losing business for their bosses. Too much bad press could cost them their jobs."

She nodded. "That make sense."

"It's about the only thing about this that does."

She smiled. "Are you talking about the case or what we did last night?" she asked.

Thinking about what they did had him taking a step toward her, almost involuntarily.

But she held up her hand, palm facing him, like she'd done with the puppy.

"Wait or stay?" he asked her.

"You have to go," she reminded him. "And last night was to get rid of the distraction of whatever this is between us."

"Something-something," he said.

"What?"

"That's what your grandfather called it," he shared. "That's why he told me where to find you."

Her face flushed. "Oh, Grandpa…" she murmured.

"You're right," Fletcher said. "He is cooler than I am."

"Yes, he is," she agreed with a smile. "And I should go, too, back to the cottage to check on him."

"And I should go," Fletcher repeated. But he really didn't want to leave her and not just because he was worried about her safety.

But if he stayed, he was going to have to worry about *his* safety. He had to leave before he really started falling for her. Because her cool grandfather had already warned Fletcher that she wasn't going to settle down anytime soon.

Not that Fletcher wanted her to. He never wanted to settle down either. All he really wanted was to do his job and catch the Slasher.

He had a feeling that he'd been close to doing that last night, but the man had escaped. And Fletcher had nearly drowned. "I have to ask you something, Kiki," he said.

She tensed. "If it's about last night, you were probably right. It was a bad idea."

He sucked in a breath, feeling like she'd punched him. "That's not what I was going to ask you about," he said.

Her face flushed. "Then what?"

"Troy. Is he left-handed?"

Her forehead furrowed as if she was trying to remember and then she nodded. "Yes, I think he is. Why?"

"Because the Slasher is, too."

"She's fine," Ruby said as she lifted Fancy down from her exam table and placed her on the floor of the medical office area of Crosswinds Training Center.

Kiki released a shaky breath of relief. After the

puppy's run-in with Troy last night, she'd been worrying about her. She and Grandpa fostered puppies to help them, not hurt them. "That's good."

"How are you?" Ruby's green eyes narrowed slightly as she studied Kiki's face, but not with that same unnerving intensity that Fletcher did.

Fletcher.

Just thinking of him had a rush of heat flashing through her body. He was such an incredible lover. Last night, or this morning—whatever time it had been—had turned out to be more than a distraction. But like she'd told him earlier this morning, it had been a bad idea. Because, after how incredible it had been between them, she was afraid that she was going to want to do it again. And again.

"I'm—I'm fine," Kiki said.

Ruby's eyes narrowed. "I hate to say this because I was sick of hearing it myself, but you look kind of tired."

Kiki was well aware of the dark circles beneath her eyes. "It was a late night at the club," she said, which was the truth. But she knew that Fletcher wanted to keep the attack as quiet as he could, so she wouldn't share that with his sister. She also didn't want to worry Ruby. The pregnant woman had already been through enough.

"Is that all?" Ruby asked.

"Yes."

"Because I heard about those attacks outside some nightclubs," Ruby said. "And I've been worried about you."

"The victims have all been men," Kiki said. "So I'm

safe." She wasn't worried about her life. She was worried about her heart.

Not that she was going to give it to Fletcher. She was too busy, and he certainly was as well. Last night was not going to be repeated. A pang of disappointment hit her, but she ignored it.

Instead of looking relieved, Ruby's face tensed with concern. "Mom said Fletcher didn't come home last night."

"I'm sure he wasn't attacked," Kiki said, wanting to reassure her friend, who'd already been through too much, but also not reveal why she was so certain.

"I know," Ruby said. "He's probably fine. He's a really good detective. He's obsessed with work. Maybe too obsessed. The reason he didn't come home was undoubtedly because he was working all night. So there must be something criminal going on again in Owl Creek." She shuddered. "I was just hoping the danger was all behind us now."

"He's a detective," Kiki gently reminded her friend. "He's always going to be working some case or another."

"He wouldn't have stayed out all night unless it was something serious, though," Ruby said.

Kiki shrugged. "Or maybe he's seeing someone." He'd certainly seen a lot of her the night before. Or actually morning.

Ruby laughed and shook her head. "I doubt that. He's only been back a little while. And with the funeral and staying with Mom, he wouldn't have had time to meet anyone. Unless…" She looked at Kiki almost hopefully.

Kiki bit her tongue so that she wouldn't say any more. Fletcher didn't want anyone to know about the Slasher, so he probably wouldn't want his sister to know he'd gone undercover with Kiki to investigate. He'd also gone undercover with Kiki last night, but that had been for an entirely other reason, for pleasure. Heat rushed to her face and her body, just as it had last night.

"It's probably for the best if you two don't get involved," Ruby said.

Kiki fought hard to maintain a neutral expression, to give nothing away about how involved she'd gotten with Ruby's brother.

The veterinarian continued, "Fletcher has never had good luck with relationships."

"Why's that?" Kiki asked as if she was only mildly curious and not wildly so.

Ruby sighed. "He's too much like Dad maybe. Throws himself into his work and doesn't leave time for anything else."

"Seems like I remember another Colton doing the same thing," Kiki teased.

"Ditto, my friend," Ruby said. "You're so busy yourself, always going from city to city, living your dream."

"Chasing it," Kiki murmured. She needed to make a few more connections. Maybe this fall, once fishing season was done and she returned to LA. Maybe there she would find the connection to get a record label interested in her music.

Or maybe she needed to spend some time in Nashville or Detroit.

She could find the connections she needed there, too. Probably anywhere but Owl Creek. But the connections she had here were for her heart. Grandpa. And Ruby.

And Fancy.

"Thanks for checking her out for me," Kiki said.

"What did you think happened to her?" Ruby asked. "She seems fine, if just a little tired like you are." The puppy had passed out in a corner of the exam room.

"She was eating leather again," Kiki said, omitting the fact that Troy might have kicked her. Or done something else that had made her yip in pain like she had.

She definitely hadn't known her assistant very well at all. What if Fletcher's suspicions were right and he was the Slasher? Would she be able to forgive herself for not realizing sooner how dangerous the man was?

Maybe she would have saved some of the victims from disfigurements—or worse if the one she'd found last night hadn't made it.

Maybe that was why she'd wanted Fletcher so badly last night. Because she hadn't wanted to think about any of the horrible things that were going on.

She'd certainly forgotten for a while.

And she'd gone to the houseboat because she'd thought she wouldn't be able to sleep. But she'd slept in Fletcher's arms. She'd felt safe.

But that was kind of ironic given that she might have the most to fear from him if she did something stupid. Like fall for him.

Because his sister had made it very clear how badly Fletcher sucked at relationships. Not that her track record was any better.

She'd never found anyone who'd been supportive of her dreams and not critical. She'd never found anyone who was willing to work around her crazy schedule. She'd never found anyone who'd loved her besides her grandfather and her friends.

"Are you sure you're all right?" Ruby asked with concern.

Kiki nodded. "Yes, just tired. Like Fancy. Now that I know she's okay I'll be able to get some sleep." But she wondered if she would without Fletcher's arms around her, holding her close.

But that was just because of what had happened. She'd needed the distraction of sex with him and the comfort of his closeness so that she could forget about the Slasher for a little while.

But when she carried Fancy out to her SUV and opened the passenger's door, she noticed a piece of paper lying on the floor that she hadn't noticed before.

She opened it up and noticed, from the direction of the cursive, that a left-handed person had written the note: *I am not the Slasher.*

Troy.

He must have slipped it inside her vehicle last night or this morning. He'd realized he was a suspect. Or he was defensive because he was guilty.

And maybe Fletcher was right. Maybe she was in more danger than she thought from the Slasher. Because if she knew who he was, he might consider her a threat.

Chapter 15

The club closed for a week, under the guise of maintenance, after Kiki had found the latest victim. This had been a good thing for Fletcher because he hadn't had to worry about maintaining his cover. If he hadn't already been compromised…

One of the other officers or techs who'd shown up at the scene might have slipped up and revealed that he was not really a suspect. That he was actually running the investigation into the Slasher. He would know when the club reopened in a couple of days.

But his cover wasn't all he had to worry about losing, though. He'd lost his objectivity and his resolve, too. He needed to be focused on finding the Slasher, not on Kiki. But despite working hard to find out all he could about Troy Hoover, Bart Taylor and Dan Sullivan, he hadn't been able to stop thinking about her.

About what they'd done.

About how damn amazing it had been, and *she* was.

She'd dropped off the note Troy Hoover had left in her vehicle, probably when it had been parked at the marina. Hopefully not while she'd been at Crosswinds.

Hopefully Troy was not following her around, but if he was, at least he knew that she'd gone to the police with his note instead of blindly accepting his word that he wasn't the Slasher.

Fletcher hadn't been at the station when she'd brought the note by. After going home to change clothes, he'd made the drive to the hospital in Conners where Greg Stehouwer, the Slasher's latest victim, was still lying in a coma. Not wanting to blow his cover, Fletcher had avoided the waiting room where the victim's family was and had only spoken with the doctor who hadn't been able to tell Fletcher anything but that the prognosis wasn't good.

The Slasher's attacks might have escalated to murder, just as Fletcher had feared they would. And so, he'd spent the past few days trying to find out as much as he could about all his suspects.

But he couldn't help but think that he was missing something. Or maybe he was just missing *someone*. Kiki. Despite how tired he should have been, he wasn't sleeping well because he wanted to sleep with her.

To get some perspective on his case, and maybe on his life, he'd stopped by Book Mark It, his sister Frannie's bookstore café. The long three-story building on Main Street squeezed narrowly between other buildings. This one was all exposed brick and cement floors. Until the Slasher had struck in Conners, he'd been spending a lot of time there because there hadn't been much else to do.

Frannie bustled around, working the café and the book counter, serving drinks and suggesting book choices to her patrons.

His sister was in her element, like Kiki was in the club. Frannie didn't quite have the adoring fans that Kiki had, though. Nobody screamed her name and tried to grab her, except for an older lady customer who gave her a hug over the loss of their dad.

After she was released, Frannie blinked furiously, clearing a rush of tears from her hazel eyes. Fletcher flinched over the twinges of concern and guilt that struck him. He should have been checking in more with his family, making sure that they were all doing okay after Dad's death. The first week, he'd stopped by the bookstore often, but he and Frannie hadn't really talked about Dad. Just his boring cases.

He hadn't checked on his other siblings. And even though he lived with his mom, he hadn't been seeing much of her either with the long hours he'd been working. So much for staying there to be a comfort for her.

He hadn't been a comfort to anyone.

As Frannie walked to the door, Fletcher glanced around the shop. He wanted to talk to his sister, but he didn't want anyone else to overhear them. About their recent loss or about his case.

Fletcher had noticed a man sitting in the corner

when he'd first walked into the store. While he didn't know the guy's name, Fletcher recognized him from his other visits to Book Mark It. He'd been here before, planted in a corner, reading a book. Even sitting down, it was easy to see that the guy was tall, with his long legs stretched out in front of him. He had a book open, but it was almost as if he was using it to hide behind instead of to read. The guy was still there, and he seemed to be watching Frannie even more intently than Fletcher had been.

Maybe the stranger kept coming around because he was interested in the bookstore owner. Frannie was pretty, with golden highlights in her hair and hazel eyes that sparkled. But there was something about the way the stranger seemed to be watching, but not wanting to be seen, that unsettled Fletcher. And it wasn't just brotherly protectiveness gnawing at him, but police instincts.

He tried to get a better look at the guy's face. But the book blocked most of it. He only lowered it when Frannie walked back from the door, and the guy's dark eyes focused on her again. He had dark hair, too, cut very short, which seemed at odds with the scruff on his face. Some gray was mixed in that scruff, so he was probably older than Frannie's twenty-six. Maybe older than Fletcher, too.

"Looking for a book?" Frannie asked him as she nudged Fletcher's arm. "Or a tall coffee?"

"Looking for my favorite sister," he said.

She smiled and replied, "Ruby isn't here."

"I'm not looking for Ruby."

"Hannah isn't here either," she said, her smile widening as she teased him.

He chuckled. "You know you're my favorite." They'd grown up sharing their love of mysteries. While Frannie had looked for hers in books, though, Fletcher looked for them in real life.

"Shh," Frannie told him. "We're not supposed to have favorites. That's what Mom has told us."

"That's because there are so many of us, especially if you include our cousins." Which their mom always had after her flighty sister had taken off and abandoned her husband and her kids. "And we all know who her favorite is now."

"Lucy," Frannie said, her voice warm with affection for their niece. "Mom loves being a grandma, which is a good thing with Ruby and Sebastian going to have a baby."

"At least something good came of that whole ordeal," Fletcher murmured, thinking of the danger Ruby had been in, similar to the danger that he might be putting Kiki in.

Since she'd found that note from Troy, he had an officer making frequent drive-bys of Jim's cottage and the houseboat. If Troy saw that cop car, maybe he would keep his distance.

If Troy was the Slasher...

"How is Mom doing?" Frannie asked with concern.

Fletcher shrugged. "She seems fine when I see her, but I really don't see that much of her."

"Is that because you're too busy or because she is?"

Fletcher shrugged. "I don't know what she's been doing, honestly."

"So *you've* been busy," she said.

Fletcher nodded. "Still doesn't excuse my not being by more to check on you."

She raised her hands. "On me? Why?"

"We just lost our dad, Frannie."

"Yes, *we*," Frannie said. "We all did. And Mom lost a husband. And I should be checking up on her myself instead of asking you how she is."

"Stop being so hard on yourself," Fletcher said. "Looks like you're busy with your own business here."

Frannie gazed around her shop, and her chin lifted with obvious pride. "Yes. I love it."

"I can tell," he said. Just like Kiki loved what she did as well. But what Kiki did was going to keep leading her away from Owl Creek. If anything ever happened to Jim Shelton, she would probably stop coming back altogether.

"How about you?" Frannie asked. "Do you love your job, Fletcher? Solving mysteries for real?"

He glanced again to that man in the corner. Was he close enough to hear them? He leaned closer to his sister and whispered, "What's that guy's story? He seems a little stalkerish."

Frannie laughed. "No. He's a regular. He's harmless."

If she really believed that, Frannie hadn't given the guy much of her usual attention. Because there was something *off* about him, and usually she would have picked up on that.

"Stop," she said.

He tensed. "What?"

"Stop being so intense and suspicious of everyone, Fletcher."

"Occupational hazard," he reminded her.

She laughed. "You were always like that. Every date Ruby, Hannah or I brought home got the third degree from our big brothers. But you were the hardest on them."

"I wasn't hard enough on Owen," Fletcher said. Hannah's deadbeat husband had abandoned her and their daughter before Lucy's first birthday.

Frannie nodded and gave a fake shiver. "That's why we're smart, staying single and all."

Fletcher nodded. But staying single didn't sound as smart as it once had to Fletcher, not since that incredible experience he'd had with Kiki, and that hadn't been just what they'd done in her bedroom on the boat. He'd even had fun shopping with her. "I wish I was smarter," Fletcher said.

"Tough case?" Frannie asked. "I can make us some cappuccinos and help you figure it out."

He was tempted. He would love a sounding board about the case. But he was waiting for information back on Bart Taylor and Dan Sullivan, seeing if they had been present at the times and places of the Slasher's other attacks. Troy had been around for at least one other of them. Two, actually, for a total of three times.

He'd been in Salt Lake City and had found the victim. Then Conners. And he'd admitted to Kiki that he'd been at Club Ignition where Greg Stehouwer had been left for dead, not just disfigured.

Had that attack escalated because Troy knew he was a suspect and that the police were closing in on him?

Or was Fletcher's other instinct right and he was missing something? He glanced again to that man sitting in the corner, and he narrowed his eyes to glare at him. "Are you sure he's harmless?"

"Fletcher!" Frannie exclaimed, her face flushing with embarrassment. "Don't scare away my customers."

"Want me to make sure that's all he is?" he asked. "What's his name?"

Frannie shook her head. "No. I'm not giving it to you. Aren't you staying busy enough in Owl Creek? Already bored with a smaller police department?"

Fletcher thought of that other night, in Kiki's bed, in Kiki's arms. "I'm definitely not bored," he said. And that had nothing to do with his case.

Kiki was being followed. She wasn't a fool. She hadn't missed that vehicle driving by her house. Past her grandfather's charter business and the boathouse. Even slowing down in front of the club when she'd checked on her equipment.

And she knew who it was.

Or at least who was responsible for it.

Fletcher had undoubtedly asked an officer to keep an eye on her. Was it for her sake though? Or was he just trying to catch Troy?

He hadn't called or texted her since that morning on the boat, so he was probably just trying to catch Troy. The Slasher.

Were they one and the same?

Kiki shuddered to think that she might have been known someone so long and been working that closely with someone capable of such violence. Uneasy now, she glanced around her as she stood at Fletcher's front door. Had the officer followed her here?

The door opened, and she jumped, startled.

"Kiki," Mrs. Colton said with a smile. "What a lovely surprise."

"I'm sorry," Kiki said. "I should have called first." She hadn't wanted to call Fletcher since he hadn't reached out to her first. But she should have called Jenny before just dropping by.

"You are always welcome," Jenny assured her. "And it's always lovely to see you." She reached out and hugged Kiki.

And Kiki, who could barely remember her mother, felt a pang of jealousy for Fletcher. Then she remembered that he'd lost his father. Jenny had lost her husband.

"I'm stopping by for two reasons," Kiki admitted. "I know you have a ton of family, but if you'd like help with anything that might be hard for them to deal with, I'd be happy to step in."

Jenny's brow furrowed with confusion so Kiki explained, "Like cleaning out closets for instance. Grandpa still had so many of Grandma's clothes in his closet when I first moved in with him that I didn't realize she was dead for the longest time. I thought she was just gone on a trip."

Mrs. Colton smiled. "That's sweet, and I expect that

he might have wanted to think that, too. Maybe that's why he kept her things for so long."

Kiki held up her hands, indicating she would back off. The bag from a shoe store dangled from one of her hands, though, the box bumping against her arm. "I'm sorry. If you're not ready, I totally understand. It hasn't been that long."

Jenny shook her head. "No, it's not that. I've already taken care of Robert's things."

Kiki had no idea what that meant. Had she tossed everything out? Or maybe she'd given his things to their sons.

"I'm sorry. I didn't mean to overstep," Kiki said. God, if Jenny told Fletcher about this, he would think she was stalking him.

"Please stop apologizing, Kiki."

Heat flushed her face with embarrassment. She was acting like a fool. Like the mother of the boy she liked had caught them making out or something.

She was being ridiculous. But being here, after being with Fletcher, unnerved her. Her offer to help Jenny had been a sincere one. But she was beginning to wonder about her own motives now. Had she just hoped to run into Fletcher while she was here, at the house where he was staying?

Had she missed him, so she was being pathetic and hoping to catch a glimpse of him?

She had another gig at Club Ignition this weekend, just a couple of days away, so she would see him then. Unless he'd chosen to pursue his investigation a different way than going undercover.

"You're not overstepping, Kiki," Jenny assured her. "I appreciate the offer so very much. Come inside, and we can visit."

Kiki's stomach flipped with nerves at the thought. She would have had a reason to be inside if she'd been helping Jenny with something. But since she'd refused, Kiki needed to gracefully extradite herself before Fletcher came home. Not that he wouldn't realize she'd been here when his mom gave him what Kiki had bought for him.

Why hadn't she thought this out more thoroughly before she'd decided to do this? Why hadn't she considered how it might look to Fletcher and to his mother?

This was a bad idea. But she found herself going inside, because she couldn't come up with an excuse. While Jenny poured them iced teas in the kitchen, she glanced over at the bag Kiki had sat on the counter.

"Is that for me?" she asked.

Kiki was tempted to press the cold glass of tea against her face. "This is actually for Fletcher," she admitted.

Instead of being offended, Jenny let out a breath of relief. "Good. I received so many lovely flowers and cards and casseroles, but I would just like life to get back to normal now."

Maybe that was why she'd already gotten rid of her husband's things. Or dealt with them somehow.

"I'd like everyone to stop worrying about me," Jenny continued, then her face flushed. "I'm sorry. That sounds rude."

Kiki shook her head and assured her, "No. I totally

get it. You're used to taking care of other people." As a nurse and as a mom and doting aunt. She was more comfortable in the role of caregiver.

"And nobody needs to take care of me," Jenny said. "I'll be fine."

"You will," Kiki said. "I've always admired how strong you are."

Jenny reached across the counter and squeezed her hand. "You're the strong one, Kiki. You've already been through so much, but you put yourself out there, in those big clubs, pursuing your dream. That takes a lot of guts."

Pride suffused Kiki, but she shrugged off the praise. "That's not difficult for me. It would be harder giving it up than going on." That was true. Music was such a part of her life. She couldn't ever give it up. For anyone.

Jenny glanced at the shoe store bag with curiosity and confusion. "So you brought this for Fletcher?"

It didn't make very much sense to Kiki now either. But Fancy had chewed up his boots. And he'd hated them so much that she'd been determined to replace them.

"I didn't even realize you two knew each other very well," Jenny said.

"We don't," Kiki said. "Not really."

And he obviously hadn't told his mother about his investigation. "We just ran into each other, and the puppy I'm fostering damaged one of his boots. I just wanted to make sure it was replaced."

"I'm sure Fletcher wouldn't expect you to do that," Jenny said. "He doesn't care much about material things. Just his career." She uttered a soft sigh.

Maybe she'd compared him to his father.

Though she was close friends with Ruby, Kiki wasn't around Owl Creek enough to understand all the personal dynamics of the Colton family.

Jenny's forehead furrowed with concern for her son. "I'm worried about him. He works so hard that even though he lives here, I barely see him." She let out another sigh, this one a bit shakier than the last. "I hate to think that there is that much crime in Owl Creek to keep him as busy as he's been lately."

He'd been successful in keeping the Slasher's latest attacks out of the news. But it was only a matter of time before someone leaked the stories. Then Jenny was going to be even more worried about her detective son.

As worried as Kiki was. Because she'd seen firsthand how vicious the Slasher was.

What the hell was wrong with this town? Why was there no mention, anywhere, of the attacks? Social media in the area had commented some about a mugging in Conners and a bar fight in the parking lot of Club Ignition. The gossips in the local gathering spot, Hutch's Diner, had been spreading the same rumors. Of muggings and bar fights.

There had been no mention of the Slasher. Not that the Slasher could take credit for everything that had happened.

But wasn't copycatting the highest form of compliment? Or maybe someone else was wanting to get some attention.

Either way, it hadn't worked.

Was trying to hide the truth some new police strategy? Had someone profiled the Slasher and figured out how necessary attention had become to them?

And now they were trying to cut it off?

The Slasher would show what they thought of that. And whoever had put the gag order on the media was going to damn well regret what they'd done.

Chapter 16

Greg Stehouwer wasn't coming out of his coma. At least that was what his doctors believed. His head injury was so severe. The doctors had advised his family to pull the plug. The Slasher would be a killer.

Fletcher felt sick that he hadn't managed to stop whoever the hell it was before it had escalated to murder, just like he'd feared it would. When he showed up at the hospital to speak to the medical examiner who had agreed to inspect the wounds on Greg's face and chest, one of the family spotted him.

"It's you!" the man yelled. "You're the one who got in the fight with him. Why aren't you in jail?" The man looked a lot like his brother with fine blond hair, blue eyes and the same athletic build.

Fletcher pulled out his badge. "No. I'm the one in

charge of this investigation. And I am so sorry about your brother." Sorrier than this man would ever know.

The guy stammered, "But—but you're the one who fought with him—"

Fletcher shook his head. "I never went out to the parking lot. I didn't leave when your brother left. You did, though."

The man's face flushed with fury and he glanced around, as if making sure nobody had overheard them. An older couple sat together on a couch, hugging each other and crying. Probably his parents who had refused to give up hope despite the doctors' grim prognosis. They'd refused to pull the plug so far, believing he would come out of it.

"He's—he is my brother," the man said. "I wouldn't hurt him."

"Where did you go after you left?" Fletcher asked.

"We started driving back to Conners. We were going to hit the clubs there."

If the groom-to-be had acted like he had at Club Ignition, Greg probably would have gotten tossed out of them, too.

"But then Greg changed his mind. He wanted to go back to teach you a lesson."

"I never saw him again until after he'd been attacked. So you let him go back alone?"

"I have a wife and kids," the man replied. "I wasn't going to get into a fight in the club." He glanced at Fletcher's badge again. "What were you doing there that night?"

"The DJ is a friend of mine," Fletcher said.

The man's blue eyes narrowed. "You're investigating that Slasher thing, aren't you? Is that why you were there?"

Fletcher clenched his jaw. While he felt badly about what had happened to Greg Stehouwer, he didn't want to reveal too much of his investigation to this man or to the press or to the people he wanted to fool tonight in the club.

Tonight. He had to drive back to Owl Creek. Had to get dressed to play the part of Kiki's assistant. His pulse quickened at the thought of seeing her again.

He'd wanted to stop by so badly this past week or at least run into her around town. But he'd also had to work this case, had to try to follow up and find all the information he could about Troy Hoover and Bart Taylor and Dan Sullivan. His possible suspects. But he couldn't help but think he was missing someone.

The man nodded. "That's why you were there. You're trying to catch that Slasher. That's who did this, isn't it? That damn Slasher!"

"I don't know," Fletcher honestly replied.

A short while later, when he spoke with the medical examiner who had inspected the deep slashes on Greg's face and chest, he was even less certain.

"His wounds don't look the same as the other ones," the doctor said. The guy was older, with iron gray hair and a mustache. "I took photos of his injuries to compare to the injuries the other victims had sustained."

"You had no problem matching the wounds from the victim at the club in Conners to the wounds on the Slasher's other victims. But you have some doubts about this one?" The same uncertainties had been going through Fletcher's mind since Kiki had found Greg so far out in the club parking lot and with such a serious head wound. One that had essentially killed him, if the doctors were right and he was brain-dead.

The medical examiner lowered his voice to a whisper and told Fletcher, "My preliminary assessment is that blade seems to have been duller and maybe a little wider. Plus, the angle doesn't match the others."

"So a different weapon?" Or a different assailant?

The guy shrugged. "I don't know yet. To say conclusively, I'll need to compare these wounds more closely to the photos taken of the other victims. If you want to wait around..."

Fletcher glanced at his watch. If he didn't hurry, he was going to be late getting to the club. Most of Kiki's equipment was still there, so she wouldn't need his help loading and unloading it until later tonight. But he needed to see her.

Hell, he'd needed to see her all week, but he'd forced himself to stay away, in case Troy Hoover was watching. The officer checking on her hadn't noticed anyone suspicious hanging around, though.

So she'd been safe.

And she had to stay that way. But going back to the club was dangerous. So would telling her not to do the job she loved, though.

Fletcher didn't want to get between her and her music. He just wanted to get between her and the Slasher.

"Call me later with what you find out," he told the medical examiner. "I have somewhere I need to be."

And someone he desperately wanted to see again. She'd bought him boots.

His mother had thought the gesture was sweet on her part, but she didn't know how much he hated those boots. Kiki did. Was it a joke? Or revenge for his not calling or texting her all week?

God, he was a coward. He hadn't known what to say to her or how to act. And knowing she was as averse to relationships as he was, he hadn't wanted to act like they were a couple, even though...

No. He had no time for relationships. A man was essentially dead now. Fletcher had to focus all his energy on finding his killer and making sure that nobody else got hurt.

Hopefully tonight ended without another victim or casualty. But Fletcher had a bad feeling about it, especially when he walked into the club and found Dan Sullivan inside already, arguing with the bartender.

"You have to give this up—" the bartender cut himself off when he noticed Fletcher. "What the hell are you doing here?"

Fletcher pointed toward the DJ booth. "Checking to make sure all of Kiki's stuff is still in the right place, so she'll be all set when she gets here." He'd had to rush to beat her there. Thankfully Mom hadn't been home when he'd run in and changed into Kiki-approved club clothes and those new boots.

"Nobody touched her stuff," Bart said, defensively.

"Are you sure?" Fletcher asked. "The bag I left up there went missing that night." With the glass that had Bart Taylor's prints on it inside. He looked pointedly at

Dan Sullivan. "Seems like people can come and go here pretty freely."

"I guess so," Bart said. "Figured you would have been arrested for what happened to that guy in the parking lot."

Fletcher tensed, wondering if the bartender knew just how seriously Stehouwer had been wounded. He shook his head. "Kiki backed me up that I never went out to the parking lot."

The older man snorted. "Of course she would back you up."

"Some security footage did, too," Fletcher said. "Never showed me going out there."

"The camera at the front door doesn't reach that far out into the parking lot, and there aren't any farther out there," Bart said. "You kept going out to the alley that night."

Was that why Stehouwer had been attacked in the parking lot? Because the Slasher had noticed how frequently Fletcher had been checking their usual crime scene?

"You could have walked out through the alley to the parking lot," Bart said.

"Seems like you really want me to be guilty of this," Fletcher said, "and I thought we were going to be friends." He glanced from one to the other of them, wondering what they'd been arguing about. "Just like you two are friends." They hadn't acted like it the other night.

But Bart had known a lot about Sullivan. Maybe they were more than customer and bartender. Bart shook his head. "He's just asking me to help him find someone."

Dan's daughter.

But was she anywhere to be found?

Fletcher had turned up a couple of Jane Does that might have been matches for the girl. Deceased.

He wasn't going to say anything to the desperate father until he could confirm it, though. He really needed the guy's DNA. And Bart's.

If only the Slasher had ever left any behind. But they hadn't left anything that would have proved their guilt.

"There are no cameras in the parking lot," Fletcher repeated back to the man. "But there are some inside here." He pointed toward the ones hidden up among the lights in the tall ceiling that had been painted black like the brick and metal walls.

The bartender shrugged. "I gave all that footage to the police."

Liar.

But if Fletcher called him that, Bart and Dan would realize that the only way Fletcher could know what he'd turned over was because he'd seen what had been turned over to the police. They'd gotten the parking lot footage and some from maybe one camera inside, but there was more than one. So why hadn't the guy turned it over?

What was on it that he'd been trying to hide? And how the hell was Fletcher going to be able to get a look at it?

Kiki had no idea if Fletcher was even going to show up at the club. Maybe he'd decided to go another direction with his investigation. Maybe he was worried that his cover had been blown the other night.

Or maybe...

He just didn't want to see her again after what had happened. Not that she cared. Sure. It had been hot. Pretty incredible.

But that didn't mean they should do it again. Maybe it meant that they shouldn't. That they couldn't risk getting used to that level of passion and pleasure.

Kiki already had a playlist together in her head. Nobody had sent her any special requests this week. Not even her girls, Janie, Claire and Amy. They'd messaged her to make sure the club would be reopened, but that had been it, which was weird.

Usually Claire asked for a few slow ones. And Amy wanted the music without the lyrics. Janie was the one after Kiki's heart and usually requested all the ones about female empowerment. Beyoncé and Joan Jett and Aretha Franklin and even The Chicks. Janie was going to be happy tonight because Kiki had gone really old school and queued up some Nancy Sinatra. *These boots...*

That had been more for Fletcher, though, if he showed up in those boots she'd bought for him. Even though she didn't have much equipment to carry in, she arrived a little early. Just to make sure everything was set up how she liked it and to get her new playlist perfected. Not because of Fletcher.

But when she walked in and found him standing at the bar, her heart did a little flippy thing in her chest, like Fancy when Kiki tried to get the puppy to follow the Spin command. She tried to ignore it and him, like he'd ignored her this past week.

"Ah, Kiki's pissed at you, too," Bart remarked.

"Nobody has any reason to be pissed at me," Fletcher said, but he didn't sound very convincing, like he didn't quite believe it himself. "Kiki, tell them that you weren't lying when you gave me an alibi the other night."

"What?" she asked. "Why would I lie about that?"

"Because you two are a little closer than you and Troy ever were," Bart called back to her.

She shrugged. "Yeah, we're old friends. So there's no way he would have left that guy out there for me to find." She didn't have to fake the shudder that swept over. "And if he had, he wouldn't be here right now. He'd be in the hospital, too. I was mad when he interfered on the dance floor. You think I would condone him doing something like *that*?"

Bart and Dan Sullivan both shook their heads and laughed. "Sorry," Bart said.

And she didn't know if the bartender was apologizing to her or to Fletcher. Then he set up a mug of coffee on the bar in front of the undercover detective and made it clear.

"I didn't mean to give you such a hard time," Bart said. "With all this crazy Slasher business, everybody who works in clubs and all the owners have been on edge. I had to talk the manager into reopening Club Ignition tonight. She wasn't sure she wanted to."

"Is that why Troy hasn't been around?" Dan asked Kiki, walking across the floor toward her. "The Slasher scared him off?"

Or he *was* the Slasher.

That was what Fletcher believed.

She nodded. "Yeah, he was freaked out. He was at that club in Salt Lake City and the one in—"

"Hey, hon," Fletcher interjected as he rushed over to her with that coffee in his hand. Obviously he still needed his caffeine to stay up late. He set the mug on top of one the speakers and asked, "What do you want me to help you with?"

Kiki realized she'd probably been about to say too much. Did Fletcher consider Dan a suspect, too? Or Bart? Her?

As a detective, he probably automatically thought the worst of everyone he met. Maybe that was why he hadn't called or texted this week.

Maybe he hadn't known if he could trust her.

She narrowed her eyes at him in a bit of a glare. "I got this, *hon*."

He grinned. "Good thing the equipment is already here. I have another new pair of boots to break in..." He raised his foot, holding up one of the work boots she'd bought him. He'd laced them a little looser, maybe in case he went into a lake again and had to get them off fast.

She hoped he didn't go in the water again. But she felt a bit like she was drowning as she stared at him, desire overwhelming her. With the boots, he wore another pair of distressed jeans. A white tank top type of undershirt underneath a light flannel jacket. And his hair was still a little damp from what must have been a quick shower. He looked sexy as hell, like one of the rock stars whose posters she'd hung on her bedroom walls growing up.

She'd like Fletcher in her bedroom again but not on the wall. Maybe holding her up against it.

His green eyes dilated, as if he was feeling the same overwhelming attraction that she was. She'd really thought that making love with him would remove the distraction. They wouldn't have to wonder anymore how it would be because they would know.

But now that they knew…

She just wanted to do it again.

He jumped over the barricade to join her in the small confines of the overcrowded booth. And her pulse quickened with his nearness, with the heat and hardness of his body so close to hers.

"Thanks for the boots," he said, and he leaned down as if he was going to kiss her.

She pulled back slightly. "I just didn't want you to sue me, you know, over my dog destroying your boots."

"You're claiming Fancy as yours?"

She shrugged. "For the moment. Just fostering her." But she was getting more attached than she'd been to the other puppies she and her grandfather had fostered. Just as she was getting more attached to…

She tensed at the thought she didn't even dare let herself fully formulate. "And don't go reading anything into me dropping off those boots," she continued, lowering her voice to a whisper. "I know that the other night wasn't anything special. Just a one-off, a hookup, a release of all that—"

He closed the distance between them and pressed his mouth against hers, kissing her deeply, passionately. When he finally raised his head, she couldn't think at all.

She could only feel. How very badly she wanted him. But had it been real at all? Or just part of his cover?

"Why did you do that?" she whispered.

"Because I really, really wanted to," he said.

"I thought it was a bad idea," she reminded him of what he'd said last weekend and that had been even before they'd made love.

"It still is," he said, "because now I want you even more, and I know it's going to be even harder for me to stay away from you."

"Why do you want to stay away from me?" she asked. Was he worried about falling for her like she was beginning to worry about falling for him?

"Because I don't want you in danger," he said.

She wanted to argue that she wasn't in any danger. But it had been strange the way that Troy had showed up on the houseboat and then how he'd left that note in her vehicle. He must have shoved it through the window or something because she always locked it.

But even if Troy wasn't the Slasher and she wasn't in any physical danger, she was in danger of another kind. Because when Fletcher had kissed her, she hadn't wanted him to stop.

Chapter 17

The weekend had passed without incident, unless Fletcher considered what had happened after the club, later that night. How he'd gone home with Kiki to that houseboat again.

How they'd made love all night.

That night and the next and the next after that. Mom probably thought he'd moved out. He *had* been looking for a place of his own.

He was staying in Owl Creek, in his new position as lead detective, so he needed a house. He'd pulled up a couple that were listed online and had done the virtual tours. That was about all he had time for.

Around his investigation.

And Kiki.

She wasn't staying. She was working on music that

she'd played for him a couple of times when he'd awakened to find her working. She'd written songs to sell and songs to sing and produce on her own. She was going to be big someday soon. Bigger than Owl Creek.

So he had to protect his heart, just like he had to protect his life. Just because nothing had happened last weekend didn't mean that the Slasher had left Owl Creek. In fact, Fletcher was pretty damn certain they were still here.

Troy Hoover. Bart Taylor. Dan Sullivan. Troy had definitely had some means and opportunity to commit those crimes. Bart wasn't always tending bar here in Owl Creek. He worked other clubs, too. And Dan Sullivan had been looking everywhere for his daughter, hitting clubs all over the west coast and neighboring areas. He could have been in those other cities where the attacks had taken place.

Fletcher needed to step up his investigation even though nothing had happened last weekend.

At least nothing at the club. A lot had happened on that houseboat between him and Kiki.

But he was extra uneasy as they unloaded her equipment tonight. He had a feeling that the Slasher was going to act out again. If it was for attention, though, they had it now. Greg Stehouwer's brother, Gerard, had talked to the press, insisting that the Slasher had attacked Greg and that the police were doing nothing to find the psychopath.

Instead of being insulted over Gerard's complaint about the police, Fletcher was relieved that Gerard hadn't blown his cover. And that the man had no idea how Fletcher was working his brother's case. It hadn't become a murder yet. Though Greg was still in a coma, his parents were holding out hope that he would regain consciousness.

Fletcher wasn't as hopeful, even though the doctors had sounded a little less bleak the last time he'd checked with them. Apparently, the guy had started breathing without the ventilator.

While it was a sign of improvement, there was no guarantee that he would wake up. And even if he did, he probably wouldn't be able to help Fletcher identify the Slasher.

According to the medical examiner, the person who had attacked Greg Stehouwer wasn't the same person who had disfigured the other victims. The wounds had been too different. So, was the Slasher one person or two different people working together?

Once again, as he and Kiki carried equipment into the club, he found Bart Taylor and Dan Sullivan together at the bar, their heads bent close as they kept their voices so low nobody could overhear them. Fletcher tried. They seemed to be working on something together. When they noticed him, they jumped apart. They were definitely hiding something.

But what?

Had they figured out who and what he really was?

"Hey, Fletcher," Bart called out. "Want your usual?"

He chuckled because his usual wasn't an alcoholic drink like bartenders usually served but a cup of coffee. Strong. After how little sleep he'd gotten over the past week, he definitely needed it. He stopped at the bar to stick his finger through the handle of the steaming mug while he juggled the other equipment he carried. "Thanks."

"How about you, Kiki?" Bart asked.

"Got my usual tea and honey," Kiki said, raising her thermos.

Fletcher grimaced, remembering when he'd tried her concoction. Like a hot toddy without the whiskey and the heat, it had been lukewarm, overly sweet tea. No wonder she had so much energy all the time.

Fletcher yawned then. He really needed his caffeine. After rolling a speaker into place, he took a long sip from his mug.

"You still not used to the late nights, old man?" Kiki teased.

He chuckled and whispered, "I'm not the one who fell asleep on me last night."

Her face flushed, and her dark eyes glittered with desire. "I'm wide awake now, though. And you're not."

"Maybe because someone woke me up so early this morning," he said.

"Do you have any complaints about that?" she asked, and she ran her fingers down his chest.

Through his thin T-shirt, he could feel the heat of her touch, and his skin tingled while his heart pounded fast and hard with excitement.

"No complaints at all," he assured her. He didn't remember the last time he'd been so happy or satiated. That thought brought on a rush of guilt that swept away some of the happiness. His dad was dead. Greg Stehouwer was basically brain-dead and other men had been permanently disfigured. He had no right to feel happy, at least not until the Slasher was behind bars. Permanently.

While the last weekend had been quiet, Fletcher didn't believe that the Slasher had left Owl Creek. He or she was here. Or maybe there were two of them, like the medical examiner had speculated after ruling that Greg Stehouwer's wounds were different from the other victims.

Two people.

Like Dan Sullivan and the bartender.

Or two totally unrelated people. Maybe whoever had attacked Greg Stehouwer was hoping that the Slasher would be blamed for it. Greg was as rich and important as he'd claimed that night on the dance floor, and once he got married, he was going to get even richer with a payout of a trust from his deceased grandparents. Money was always a strong motive for murder. And whoever had attacked Greg Stehouwer hadn't been simply trying to disfigure him.

Was that what the Slasher had been doing to the other victims? Trying to ruin their lives for some reason like he or she believed theirs had been ruined?

Like Dan Sullivan.

He'd lost his daughter. Did he blame every guy he saw in a club for taking her away from him? Fletcher had sent out her picture everywhere, and he was waiting for a call back from a few coroners whose Jane Does had matched the description of Dan's missing daughter.

One was in LA. There was another in San Francisco and one in Salt Lake City.

After helping Kiki set up her equipment, Fletcher headed toward the bar where Sullivan was sitting. He set his empty mug on the granite bar for Bart to refill.

"You've been the first customer here the last couple of weekends," Fletcher remarked to Sullivan. And Bart had been letting him in before the club even opened. "Do you have a lead that your daughter is in Owl Creek?"

Dan shook his head. "No. No leads. But I think I'm starting to fall for this town. All the fishing and hiking."

"You been doing a lot of that during the week?" Fletcher asked.

The guy shrugged. "Some. It's a beautiful area. Did you grow up here?"

Fletcher tensed, wondering if his cover had been blown. Just as he'd been checking out Dan Sullivan and Bart Taylor, they might have been checking him out. Since he had grown up here, Dan and Bart could have run into a lot of people who knew him and knew what he really did for a living. And it wasn't acting as Kiki's assistant but as the lead detective for Owl Creek PD.

"I did grow up here," he admitted. There was no point in lying about that if Sullivan had already figured out the truth.

"Is that how you know Kiki?" A female voice asked the question.

And Fletcher turned, expecting to see a waitress behind him. But it was one of the women he called Kiki's superfans. He didn't know which one was which, but this one was the redhead with the frizzy hair and bright smile.

He smiled back. "Yes, it is."

"She's amazing!" one of the other ones gushed as the blonde and the brunette walked up to the bar, too.

"Doors open, huh?" Fletcher asked.

"The bouncer let us in a little early," the blonde said with a wink.

"He always lets the prettiest women in first," Fletcher said.

They giggled at his compliment. He had a soft spot for them because of their adulation of Kiki. He had become one of her superfans, too.

"Are you going to dance with us tonight?" the brunette said with a bit of a whine. And then Bart handed her a glass of wine across the bar.

"If I'm going to keep up with you ladies, I'm going to need more coffee," he said.

"I already refilled your cup," Bart said, pointing at it. "It's probably getting cold."

"Let's get this party started!" Kiki's voice echoed throughout the nearly empty club. More people were coming through the doors, but they obviously hadn't been lined up around the block like that first weekend Fletcher had gone undercover as her assistant.

Greg's brother going public about the Slasher attacking him here had definitely affected their business. The only reason anyone had probably showed up at all tonight was because of Kiki. She was amazing.

She wore the red leather vest and shorts, probably

because she'd left it on the boat that first time they'd made love and she hadn't gone back to the cottage to grab any of her other club wardrobe. This was Fletcher's favorite, though, because it reminded him of that night, though not everything that had happened then had been good.

He could have drowned. And maybe he had in a way.

He'd drowned in the pleasure she gave him. In her.

To get the dancing started, she sang along with the songs she played, mixing them between two of her four turntables. He didn't know how she kept everything straight, especially when she had to be as tired as he was.

He reached for the mug of coffee. It was getting a little lukewarm, so he drank it fast and had Bart fill it again. He had a feeling he was going to have to stay alert tonight. That something was going to happen.

Because that feeling was an uneasy one that had goose bumps lifting on his skin. And he wore a flannel shirt over his undershirt, so he shouldn't have been cold. He should have been too hot in the flannel, especially with the way Kiki looked.

Just the sight of her, her body moving to the music she played, had him a little light-headed, a little dizzy on her beauty and the sound of her husky voice singing along with that music.

He was in danger. And not just from the Slasher. He was in danger of falling for Kiki.

Kiki was so pumped with excitement that she couldn't stop dancing. The music flowed through her like her blood. She'd written some great stuff over the past week. And she'd made some incredible love with an incredible man.

A very sweet man in the way that he played with Fancy and worked with her on her commands and the way that he listened to all Kiki's songs and acted so in awe of her. Sometimes just the way he looked at her with that strangely intense look of his...

He hadn't been looking at her that way tonight, though. It was as if he could barely hold his lids up over his eyes. At the moment, he was a very tired man.

She felt a pang of regret that she'd kept Fletcher up late and then woken him up early. He was obviously tired, so tired that he'd been nearly nodding off in the booth.

So it was probably good that her girls had cajoled him into joining them on the dance floor. But he wasn't moving with his usual rhythm. He seemed sluggish, and he stumbled and nearly fell. It was almost as if...

He was drunk.

But his coffee cup sat atop the speaker, vibrating with the beat. She leaned forward and sniffed it. She didn't smell alcohol in it, though she wouldn't have expected to since she'd never seen him drink anything but coffee. But the way he was acting...

He was more than tired. It was as if he'd been drugged.

Alarm shot through her. Was that what had happened to those other men? Why they hadn't managed to fight back harder against the Slasher? Because they'd been drugged first?

She gazed out into the crowd, looking for him. But now, later in the night, the dance floor was full. She couldn't even find her girls now.

Maybe they'd taken him back to the bar. Or outside for some air.

He definitely needed it. But if he went into the alley tonight as he usually did, to check for victims, he might become the next one.

The Slasher had figured out who Fletcher really was. A Colton. Rich and spoiled like all those other victims.

After the recent death of his father, he was probably even richer. It had been easy enough to figure out who he was after just following him around for a bit, like to that bookstore his sister owned.

There were a whole lot of Coltons in this town. So if one more died, like his father had, he wouldn't be missed. Would Kiki miss him?

The Slasher felt a pang of regret. But it couldn't be helped. Kiki would realize, in the long run, that the Slasher had done her a favor.

Had saved her from that inevitable speech rich guys like Colton gave to women like her.

It was fun while it lasted, but it wasn't going to work out in the long run. They were too different.

And what they really meant was that they were better.

And they wanted someone better.

The Slasher knew what Fletcher Colton wanted. Not just someone better.

Detective Colton wanted the Slasher and he'd just been using Kiki. So really, this was a favor to Kiki. Getting rid of Fletcher Colton for good.

Chapter 18

Fletcher's head pounded, and his vision blurred, the strobe lights blinding him with blue, red and purple flashes. He needed more coffee. Or maybe some fresh air.

He'd gotten away from the girls and off the dance floor with the excuse that he needed to use the restroom. And he had…

To splash cold water on his face. But that hadn't woken him up. And when he stepped back out into the club, those lights flashed at him, making his head pound harder than the music. The music.

Kiki. He needed to talk to Kiki. To tell her something…

But he couldn't think any clearer than he could see. He moved back into the bathroom, where the lights didn't flash, just buzzed overhead from the fluorescent bulbs. That light was harsh but shouldn't have made him feel as dizzy and light-headed as he felt.

Maybe he needed air.

His stomach roiled, too, though. And he stepped into a stall to use the toilet bowl as his stomach expelled everything he'd eaten and drank that day. Just coffee.

So why was he so tired? So light-headed?

Maybe his blood sugar was too low. Or…

He reached into his pocket for the handkerchief he'd shoved into it earlier, but paper crinkled in his fingers instead of cloth. A note.

He pulled it out and had to blink a couple of times to focus on it, to read the scrawled writing. *Looking for me? You know where to find me. If you're brave enough…*

The Slasher. He or she hadn't signed the note, but they hadn't had to. He knew who had given it to him even though he hadn't noticed when it had been shoved in his pocket. Who had passed it to him? And when?

On the dance floor?

Or when he'd been standing in the short line for the men's room? A couple of guys had pushed past him. And he'd also walked by Dan and Bart at the bar. When he'd stumbled, Dan had jumped up and helped him steady himself.

"Whoa, there, you must be burning the candle at both ends, Fletcher."

He had been. But the way he felt now was more than tired. He'd probably been drugged.

So he knew he shouldn't go out to that alley. Not

now. Not alone and definitely not in this condition. Whatever this was.

But maybe throwing up would help clear his head. And the fresh air...

Not that the air in the alley was fresh. And not that he should go out there alone.

His head had cleared enough from vomiting that he knew to call for help. He reached for his cell and sent a picture of the note to the officer who was always on standby in the area when Fletcher was working undercover at the club. His back-up would be here within minutes. Would meet him in the alley...

He left the stall, stopped to wash his hands and his face and to gulp mouthfuls of water from the faucet. Now, if he headed to the alley, the officer would certainly be almost there, too.

The alley was behind the kitchen, so that only employees were supposed to use it. Maybe that was why Fletcher hadn't found anyone out there yet when he'd worked undercover at Club Ignition.

Maybe that was why Greg Stehouwer had been attacked in the parking lot instead. But he hadn't received a note. Or if he had, it hadn't been on him when Kiki had found him.

Of course, the detail of the note hadn't been leaked to the press. And if the person who'd attacked Greg had been a copycat, they wouldn't have known that detail.

But this person, the one who'd slipped Fletcher the note, knew it. They had to be the Slasher.

He started down the hall toward the bar area and just as he neared it, he stumbled again. But Dan Sullivan wasn't there to catch him this time. He didn't see Bart either. One of the cocktail waitresses was behind the bar serving drinks.

Where had those two gone? Were they waiting in the alley for him?

And where was Kiki?

Even though music played, it wasn't with the energy and mix that she gave to the beat. He glanced across the dance floor to the booth. It was empty.

Where was she?

Hopefully in the restroom. But he had a horrible feeling she'd gone into the alley. Maybe looking for him. And she was going to find what was waiting for him.

The Slasher.

He couldn't wait for backup, not if Kiki was in danger. He had to go out there now and hope like hell that he wasn't too late.

Kiki hadn't found Fletcher. She had found someone else, though, hidden among the dancers on the floor. Troy. He'd caught her wrist when she'd tried to pass him. And she'd nearly used the pepper spray she had clasped in one hand.

"Kiki."

"Troy! What are you doing here?" Was he the one who'd drugged Fletcher? He'd had to be drugged to be as sluggish as he'd been. Because he'd been tired before but had never moved like that.

"I need your help."

She shook her head and tried to pull her wrist free of his grasp. But, like the groom from the bachelor party a couple of weekends ago, he tightened his grasp instead of releasing her. "Let me go!" she told him.

She didn't want to pepper spray him. Not there in the middle of a crowded dance floor.

Too many other people might get hurt. But she didn't want Fletcher getting hurt. Or was she already too late for that?

"You need to listen to me," Troy implored her. "I'm not the Slasher. But I think I know who is."

"That's why you need to talk to the police, Troy," she urged him. "You need to tell them what you know."

He shook his head. "They're not going to listen to me. And I don't really have any proof. You need to listen to me, Kiki. I want to tell you."

She shook her head. "I'm not the police, Troy. I can't help you with this."

"I thought you were my friend."

She shook her head again. "No. I don't even really know who you are."

He released her then, so abruptly that she stumbled back into some other dancers.

"Kiki! Kiki, play my song next."

She wasn't going to play any songs. She had to find Fletcher. She had to make sure that he was okay. She shoved her way through the other dancers, ignoring them as they tried to catch her attention, as they tried to stop her. She kept her grip tight on her can of pepper spray.

She had a feeling that she was going to need it. Either because of Troy or because of Fletcher.

He wasn't at the bar. She would have seen him, in his blue and pink flannel shirt, if he had been. He claimed to hate that shirt, just as he claimed to hate the boots that he kept so loosely laced now. But he'd worn that shirt a few times. Just to cover his holster, he claimed.

He had his gun.

The pressure on her chest eased a little with that realization. He was armed.

But if he'd been drugged, like she was worried he'd been, he might not be able to fire that weapon in time to save himself from the Slasher's attack. Because if he had been drugged, it had probably been the Slasher who'd done it.

Where would the Slasher be waiting for Fletcher? The parking lot where Greg Stehouwer had been attacked? Or the alley?

She chose to check the alley first. Because it was closer and because she could rush through it to the parking lot where she'd found Stehouwer bleeding in the weeds.

One of the waitresses who was tending the bar glanced at her as she ducked under the counter and passed through the doorway into the kitchen. A lot of employees went to the alley to smoke, but Kiki rarely went into the kitchen and definitely not into the alley unless she'd been carrying her equipment in or out through that door.

With the location of the parking lot and the front door, though, she could park by the entrance and bring her stuff in that way. But because those spots were designated for people with disabilities, she had to move it after she unloaded her equipment.

But even though she hadn't used the alley often here, she knew where it was. She rushed through the kitchen, past the enormous dishwashers that leaked steam into the room, to that steel door.

When she pushed it open, she saw Fletcher in the faint glow from the light at the top of the short stairwell that led down to the asphalt where he stood, his gun gripped in his hand. But she saw only him.

A dumpster was just below that stairwell, jammed between this old warehouse and the one next to it that was still abandoned. Nobody had renovated it yet like they had Club Ignition.

She'd thought once or twice about how it would make a great sound studio. It was all brick and metal and thick insulation. The acoustics in it were even better than in the club. But she didn't have the money for something like that—at least not yet. And right now she didn't have the interest.

All her focus was on a certain detective.

"Fletcher!" she called out to him.

He tensed, then turned slowly toward her, as if he was about to pass out. He had definitely been drugged. And as he turned, something jumped from the shadows on the other side of that big dumpster. It didn't look like a person to Kiki—who couldn't see anything but plastic, like some kind of synthetic suit with a hood and mask—but then a knife blade flashed.

And she knew who it was. The Slasher.

She screamed again. "Fletcher! Behind you!"

But the blade was already swinging toward him as he turned with the gun in his hand.

Kiki rushed down those steps as she raised her can of pepper spray. With the Slasher wearing a mask, it might not affect them at all. But Kiki had to try to protect Fletcher.

She had to make an effort to save him. Because he wasn't aiming or firing his weapon. Instead, when that blade came down across his arm, he dropped it onto the ground. And then he fell onto it, too, his blood sprayed across the asphalt beneath him.

Kiki screamed again as she rushed toward the Slasher. She pressed hard on the canister button, sending that pepper spray out toward the attacker who turned that knife on Kiki now.

Instead of saving Fletcher, Kiki might have become just another victim of the Slasher.

Chapter 19

Fletcher felt no pain from his wound being stitched, just the tug and pull of the needle moving through his skin. The cut across his forearm wasn't all that deep, but it had bled like hell, the torn sleeve of his flannel shirt saturated with blood. It continued to ooze through the stitches pulling the wound together.

At least they'd numbed the area on his arm.

His head still hurt from whatever drug had been in his coffee. A doctor at the hospital in Conners had taken a sample of his blood to test it. To see what had been slipped to him.

"This is going to take a lot of stitches," the ER doctor warned him as he continued pushing the needle through his skin like he was hemming some curtains.

Fletcher knew he was lucky that it was just his arm.

And not his face like the Slasher's other victims. Or his chest.

Or his heart.

Because he didn't think the Slasher had just intended to disfigure Fletcher. They had probably intended to kill him. If not for Kiki, they would have probably succeeded.

"Kiki Shelton. Is she here, too?" he asked, and his voice was raspy—probably from that drug. He knew he'd asked already, but his mind was still a little foggy from whatever he'd been slipped.

"Yes," the doctor replied. "She's fine."

"So she's in the waiting room?" he asked. That was the only way she would be fine. If she'd been in the ambulance with him, which was how he vaguely recalled things, then she wouldn't be fine.

He couldn't remember what all had happened in that alley. Between the drugs and then the blood loss.

And the pain.

He'd felt that then. Not just in his arm or his head. Even his eyes stung. They burned still, so much so that he lifted his free hand toward his face.

"Don't," the doctor warned him. "I'm not sure we got all the pepper spray off you. You might have some on your hand that you'll get in your eyes."

"Pepper spray?"

"Yeah, it probably saved your life," the doctor replied. "The woman who rode in with you—"

"Kiki Shelton." She had been with him. He could vaguely remember her hand on him, touching him, as if she'd wanted to make sure that he was still alive.

"She probably saved your life. She used it on the attacker, but with that alley being so narrow and the air conditioner condenser being right there, the pepper spray went all over the place."

"How is Kiki?" he asked with concern. "I'm a detective, Doctor, with Owl Creek PD. I was working undercover at that club as Kiki's assistant." And if she'd gotten hurt because of him…

"She got it the worst," the doctor admitted. "We had to flush out her eyes and then put bandages over them so that she doesn't strain them."

So she was essentially blind. Was that why she'd held onto him in the ambulance? Or had she been worried about him? She must have been, or why else would she have come out into the alley like she had?

"And the Slasher?" Fletcher asked, his voice raspy. Now he knew it was probably from the pepper spray.

"Slasher?" The doctor's hand stilled midstitch. "Is that who—of course. That's who."

"Who what? Did they come in, too?"

The doctor shook his head. "No. They got away."

Fletcher cursed.

And the doctor nodded now in agreement. "That psycho needs to be caught. I saw what they did to those last two victims."

"How is Greg Stehouwer?" Fletcher asked.

"A frickin' miracle," the doctor replied. "The neurologist said there's brain activity now. He'll probably wake up soon. But he'll still have a long road to recovery after he does."

At least he was alive. That was something.

"I see why you put yourself at risk like that to catch this sociopath," the doctor said. "You're lucky Ms. Shelton was there."

He was lucky. She wasn't. "You think she'll be all right?" he asked, his heart beating fast with fear for her. And with something else.

Something he couldn't let himself acknowledge.

The doctor nodded. "Pepper spray doesn't cause permanent blindness. Usually that lasts for up to forty-five minutes at the most. Ms. Shelton's case is a little different because I think she rubbed it in. She made it worse. But I'm sure she'll be fine."

"And she didn't get cut?" Fletcher's stomach lurched with the horror of her being harmed like those men had been.

Already the numbness in his arm was beginning to wear off and he could feel the nip of the needle, the strain of his skin, as the doctor finished closing his wound.

He didn't care about his pain, though. He just didn't want Kiki to be in pain.

"She didn't get cut," the doctor assured him.

"Where is she?" Fletcher asked. He had to see for himself that she was okay.

"We put her in an individual room in the ER area," the doctor said. "She needs to rest for a while, and then hopefully her vision will be fine and we can remove those bandages."

Hopefully.

But what if it wasn't?

If Kiki lost her vision because of him, because of

his involving her in this investigation, he would never forgive himself. And he doubted she would either.

Some rescuer Kiki was. She would stick to playing music from now on instead of playing detective. Rather than helping Fletcher, she'd probably distracted him. And he'd gotten wounded because of her instead of catching the Slasher like he'd been trying to do.

In addition to the laceration on his arm, the pepper spray had also affected him, making him cough and gag like she'd been doing.

And the burning.

It hurt so much. Even now, with the cold bandage wrapped over her eyes, her skin burned. And her throat ached from all that coughing. She needed her honey lemon tea right now more than she needed the sleep the doctor had advised her to get.

Like she could sleep at all with that image in her head. Of that person, bundled up in a hazmat suit, lunging at Fletcher with that huge knife.

It had been like a machete. So sharp.

It could have killed Fletcher easily. Or taken off his arm.

The wound had been bleeding so much. She needed to check on him more than she needed to rest her eyes. She couldn't rest without knowing how he was.

Hinges creaked as the door opened. And even through the bandage, Kiki could see a faint lightness. But then the hinges creaked again, as the door closed, shutting out the light.

"Hello?" she called out.

Had a doctor or nurse come back to check on her?

"Can you take these bandages off now?" she asked. "I'm fine. Really."

She waited a beat, but nobody responded. Had someone just opened the door and then closed it again?

But then she heard the squeak of a shoe sole against the linoleum flooring. And another sound...

Of someone breathing.

She was not alone.

"Hello?" she called out again. "Who's there?"

But only that eerie silence greeted her again. Who was it? And why wouldn't they identify themselves? Was it because they didn't want anyone to identify them? Was it the Slasher?

The Slasher's eyes burned with nearly the same intensity as their rage. Why had Kiki Shelton messed everything up? She was supposed to stay up in her damn booth, playing her music like she always did.

Except for those rare instances when she came out into the crowd. But even then, she never made it farther than the dance floor.

She shouldn't have come out to that alley. Shouldn't have interfered like that.

Fletcher Colton should have been dead. Or at least hurt a hell of a lot worse than he'd been.

He had to be the one who'd stifled the story about the attack in Conners. He'd been working that case, too. The Slasher had found that out, too.

That the lead detective of Owl Creek Police Department had been helping out in Conners. Like he'd claimed to just be helping an old friend when he'd posed as Kiki's assistant.

But maybe they were old friends. Maybe that was why it seemed like there was something between them. Something that could have cost Kiki her life.

Something that still would if she was stupid enough to get in the Slasher's way again.

Chapter 20

The hospital rushed his blood work results. His coffee had definitely been tainted with rohypnol. As out of it as Fletcher had been, he wouldn't have survived that skirmish with the Slasher in the alley if it hadn't been for Kiki and her pepper spray. She had saved his life.

The backup officer hadn't gotten Fletcher's text right away. Since Fletcher had had no issue with the cell reception when he'd called to report finding Greg Stehouwer, there must have been a cell signal jammer inside the club. Or maybe the Slasher had brought one.

It seemed as if they'd thought of everything, like the hazmat-type suit they'd worn. No wonder they never left any DNA or fingerprints at the scene.

Eventually the text had gone through, though, and the

officer had arrived and then called the ambulance that had brought him and Kiki to the hospital in Conners.

So Kiki had been his backup instead of an officer. She'd saved his life. And he had to make sure she was really all right. So even though he knew she was supposed to be resting, he wanted to check on her and had wheedled her location out of the ER doctor.

But Kiki wasn't resting. As he approached her room, he heard her voice rise, demanding to know, "Who's there? Who are you?"

He could hear the fear in her voice, too. So he pushed open the door to the darkness of the room. Only the light from the hall spilled into the space, revealing a bed and a shadow looming over it.

That shadow lunged toward Fletcher, or maybe toward the door, but he blocked them and shoved the person to the floor. Then he fumbled against the wall and turned on the light.

It illuminated the man lying on the floor. He was thin with long, stringy hair that looked like it hadn't been washed in a while. And his eyes were wild and bloodshot, like an animal that was starving for food or...

The guy tried to scramble up from the floor, but Fletcher held him down with one of those heavy boots Kiki had bought him. "Sit back, Troy. You're not getting away from me this time." And he used his cell to call for the backup that had followed him and Kiki to the hospital.

Kiki.

She sat up in the bed now, pushing at the bandage

that had been wrapped around her head. The compress dropped onto the sheet that covered her. Her eyes and skin were red, but she blinked and focused on the two men.

"Why didn't you say something, Troy?" she asked, her voice sharp with anger. "Why'd you just stand there in the dark?"

Troy lay back on the floor as if resigned, but he didn't answer her.

Then she focused on Fletcher and said, "What are you doing! You shouldn't be out of bed! You're hurt."

Fletcher would rather have her angry than afraid, even if she was angry with him. "I'm fine," he said. Thanks to her. "How are you?"

"Pissed off," she said. She pointed toward his arm. "You're still bleeding."

The bandage covering his wound was turning red with fresh blood. He must have reopened the stitches when he shoved Troy to the floor. "No reason to be mad about my cut. It's been stitched up."

"I'm mad that you went into that alley alone."

"I couldn't find you," Fletcher said.

"I couldn't find *you*," Kiki said. "And I could tell from the way you were acting that somebody must have slipped you something."

"They did," Fletcher confirmed. He looked down at Troy. "What the hell are you doing here in her room? How did you even know she was here?" Unless he was the Slasher.

"He was at the club," Kiki answered for him.

Fletcher nodded. "Of course he was. You've been

everywhere the Slasher has attacked someone, Troy. Why is that?"

"It's not me," Troy said, his voice quavering with fear, and his body started shaking so badly it seemed like he was more than afraid. He could be having a seizure, or maybe going through withdrawal. Fletcher had seen people acting similarly in his years as a police officer.

Fletcher struggled to imagine this guy as the Slasher. How would someone like him have eluded the authorities for so long in so many different places?

The organizational skills it had taken to plan and execute the attacks didn't seem like something Troy was capable of doing. The Slasher had been so careful and had made certain to leave behind no clues.

No DNA. No fingerprints.

The note. Fletcher had the note. Maybe there would be something on it since the Slasher hadn't managed to take it back like they had from the other victims.

Was that why Troy was here? But then he would have been in Fletcher's room and not Kiki's.

"What the hell are you doing here?" Fletcher asked again.

"I had to talk to Kiki," Troy said. "She has to know the truth."

"You said that you know who the Slasher is," Kiki said. "You told me that on the dance floor. Who is it, Troy?"

The guy's skinny body shook harder, as if he was convulsing.

"What's wrong?" Kiki asked.

"I think he's going through withdrawal." Fletcher stepped away to call out, "We need help!"

But then Troy was up from the floor, trying to shove past Fletcher. Fletcher caught him again and dragged him down to the floor, holding him against the linoleum. Pain throbbed in his arm and in his head. He was in no condition to subdue a suspect. And no matter what Troy claimed, he was still a suspect.

Maybe he was even faking the shakes. He was doing it again, clicking his teeth together and trembling.

"What's wrong with you?" Fletcher asked.

A nurse appeared in the doorway and gasped. "What's going on?"

"Get security."

The officer Fletcher had called stepped around the nurse. "Detective Colton, I'm sorry—"

Fletcher shook his head, forestalling another apology. The guy had been apologizing since he'd found Fletcher and Kiki in the alley. "You're here now. We need to arrest this guy."

"Is this the Slasher?" Officer Blaine asked.

Fletcher shrugged. "I don't know." And he really wasn't certain. "But he has an outstanding warrant for drug possession and another for failure to pay child support."

"We need to assess his medical condition," the nurse said. "Before you take him out of here. He appears to be having a seizure." She stepped into the hall and shouted for a doctor.

Troy's shaking body pushed against Fletcher's wounded arm, loosening his grasp. Maybe he was faking, just trying to escape. But with the officer standing inside the room now, there was no escape.

"Wait," Kiki said. She swung her legs over the side of the bed, and she joined him and Troy on the floor. She wore a thin gown instead of her club clothes. "You wanted to talk to me, Troy," she reminded the guy. "You wanted to tell me who the Slasher is."

But the guy's eyes rolled back into his head, and he convulsed even harder. And Fletcher had a feeling that he wasn't faking now.

The doctor, the one who'd stitched up Fletcher, rushed into the room then with the nurse. Fletcher and Kiki and the officer stepped back into the hall to get out of the way. But then they had to flatten themselves against the wall as the doctor and nurse rolled out a gurney with Troy on it, his body still convulsing.

"Do you really think he knows who the Slasher is?" Officer Blaine asked Kiki the question.

She shrugged. "I don't know."

"Stay here," Fletcher told the officer. "Make sure he doesn't get away. We need to arrest him for those outstanding warrants and hold him for questioning."

The officer nodded and rushed off to catch up to that gurney, leaving Fletcher and Kiki alone. Even with the red and swollen eyes and skin, she was so beautiful. He wanted to close his arms around her and hold on and never let her go. But being close to him had already put her in danger.

"I'm sorry," he said. "I never should have gotten you involved in this investigation." Unable to stop himself, he reached out and touched her face, skimming his fingers along her cheek. "I'm so sorry you got hurt."

She shivered a bit, probably cold in her thin gown. "I'm fine," she said. "But you're not. You're bleeding more now. The wound must have reopened." She pointed at his arm where the bandage had gotten saturated, and blood trickled down over his hand to drop onto the floor.

"It could have been much worse," he said. The Slasher had lured him out to the alley to do more than maim him. "You saved my life."

But it killed him that she'd been so close to the Slasher that the Slasher could have done to her what they'd done to so many other people. And he had to make sure that she was never put in that kind of danger again.

At least not because of him.

Kiki wasn't usually squeamish, but all that blood on Fletcher's arm made her light-headed. Or maybe that was still the aftereffects of the pepper spray that had gone all over her and probably all over him, too, since his eyes were scarlet and swollen like hers.

She couldn't stand and watch as the doctor unbandaged and stitched his arm, so she slipped back into the room where she'd left her bandage lying on the bed, the bandage that had covered her eyes and made her feel so helpless. She hated that feeling, hated how it brought her back to the edge of a memory she never wanted to let into her mind again.

Of her parents' accident, of being in that car with them and not able to help them. And so, she'd shut it all out with music, singing to herself until help had arrived.

But it had been too late for her parents. Just as it had almost been too late for Fletcher and for her. The siren in the distance had probably scared off the Slasher more than her pepper spray had.

The pepper spray had covered her clothes, too, so the red leather outfit was sealed into a plastic bag. She had nothing to wear home but her gown. And she wanted to go home.

She couldn't call Grandpa, though. She didn't want him to see her with her eyes and the skin around them so red and puffy. She didn't want to worry him like she was worried. The Slasher was still out there.

She didn't think it was Troy, and she didn't think Fletcher did anymore either. But he still had Officer Blaine sticking close to him, making sure he didn't escape again.

She needed to escape. She could have called Ruby to bring her some clothes and give her a ride back to Owl Creek, but she didn't want to wake up the pregnant woman at this hour. And she didn't want to worry her either.

A knock sounded at the door, and it creaked open to Fletcher. He walked inside, a bag dangling from his hand. "I had Frannie bring you some clothes," he said.

"Frannie's here?" she asked. While she knew Ruby best, from Crosswinds, she liked all of Fletcher's sisters.

"I just had her drop some stuff at the desk that you could wear home. And I had your vehicle towed here, too. The doctor said you'll be able to go home. So you can get dressed and leave."

"Trying to get rid of me?" she asked.

"Trying to get you out of danger," he said. "You never should have been in that situation tonight. It's my fault."

"It's the Slasher's fault," she reminded him.

"But still, until the Slasher is caught, you should stay away from the clubs," he said.

"Now you're really pissing me off," she said. "You have no right to tell me how to live my life."

He stared at her with that strangely intense gaze of his. "I have no right?" he asked, and a muscle twitched along his tightly clenched jaw.

Was he mad at her?

Or just mad about what had happened?

Kiki got that; she was angry, too.

She was mad at the Slasher. At Fletcher for putting himself in danger. And mostly she was mad at herself for caring so damn much about him. This was his job—catching criminals. Of course, the work could put him in danger because of the treacherous people he was determined to catch.

But after losing her mom and dad, Kiki didn't want to lose anyone else she loved. Not that she loved Fletcher.

But she could fall for him. If she wasn't careful...

She was on the verge, feeling kind of like she was balanced on the edge of a cliff, and it wouldn't take much of a push for her to fall over it. To fall in love.

The past few weeks had been amazing. In the bedroom and out of it. Fletcher was fun and funny and sweet. And sometimes the way he looked at her...

She felt like she might not be the only one on the edge of that cliff. But he was looking at her differently right now. He seemed to want to push her away from the cliff and away from him.

"You have no right to tell me I can't do my job," she said. "Any more than I have a right to tell you that you can't do yours."

That muscle twitched along his jaw again.

"You were the one who was really in danger tonight," she pointed out. "You're the one the Slasher drugged and lured to the alley. Not me."

"But you put yourself in harm's way," he said. "Because of me. If I hadn't been there…"

"I might have gotten nervous about some other guy getting hurt and followed him into the alley," she said. "So don't take it so personally, Colton."

His lips twitched now along with that muscle, as if he was tempted to grin no matter how mad he was at her. "I will take it personally if you get hurt," he said. And then almost reluctantly he added, "I don't want you getting hurt because of me, Kiki. Because of this investigation."

"The club will close down for at least another week," she said. If not permanently since another attack had taken place. She hoped that didn't happen. She really enjoyed spinning at a venue in her hometown. "So you don't have to worry about anything happening to me there."

"I will worry until the Slasher is caught," he said.

"Maybe Troy really does know who the Slasher is," she suggested.

If so, she had no doubt that Fletcher would find out. He would get the truth out of him. And then maybe all of this would be over. But to her, right now, it felt like it was already over between the two of them.

And she wasn't sure if that was because Fletcher wanted to keep her safe or if he wanted to keep himself safe from falling for her.

She could relate to that. She didn't want to love anyone else and lose them like she had her folks. Maybe it was best if it ended now before anyone got hurt any worse.

Chapter 21

Troy Hoover had recovered remarkably fast, getting released from the hospital within just a couple of days. Maybe it was the methadone he was given, or maybe he'd just been faking all along. Fletcher didn't know. And he didn't care because now that the man had been released from the hospital, he was in police custody in Owl Creek. At the moment, he was in the interrogation room with Fletcher seated across from him.

"The Slasher wants to kill me," Troy insisted.

Fletcher furrowed his brow. "Why? The other victims were all rich and were usually at the clubs for bachelor parties." Troy was neither rich nor a bachelor.

He owed child support, but he'd never officially divorced his children's mother.

"I don't know," Troy said. "Maybe he thinks I saw him or something. That I know who he is."

"If you do know who he is, then he's right about you," Fletcher pointed out. "Who is it, Troy?"

"That old guy that hangs around the bar," Troy said, his voice cracking with fear. "He even paid Bart to try to get me to come into the club. That's why I kept going in because Bart kept calling me and telling me to show up."

That explained those quiet conversations that Fletcher had interrupted between Bart and Dan Sullivan. "Why?"

Troy shrugged. "I don't know why. The only thing I can think of is he's the Slasher."

"But you have no proof of that?"

"He's real rich and real smart. I'm sure he's covered his tracks."

"Then why would he think you're a threat?" Fletcher asked. "If there's no evidence to link him to those attacks?" Sullivan wouldn't worry about the testimony of a known drug user implicating him when there was no evidence that could back up Troy's wild claim.

"I don't know." Troy yawned. It was getting late. After his release from the hospital, he'd had to be driven to Owl Creek, processed and arraigned. "I don't know."

Because Troy was a drug user and, from his doctor's report, had done some significant damage to his body, it wasn't likely that he'd been able to execute those crimes like the Slasher had. But Dan Sullivan…

He was a distinct possibility. And even Bart.

Troy had only the bartender's word that Sullivan was the one trying to lure him into the club. What if

Bart was acting on his own? Why would either of them want Troy at the club? As Fletcher had pointed out, he wasn't the Slasher's usual victim. But maybe this had nothing to do with the Slasher.

Maybe there was another reason they'd wanted Troy at the club. Who knew? Maybe he owed Bart the bartender some money. Fletcher wasn't as concerned about Troy as he'd once been, so he stood up and stepped out of the interrogation room. "He can go back to his cell," Fletcher told an officer. He was still wanted on those other warrants and had to make whatever bail the judge had set for him.

Having shut off his phone while he was in the interrogation, Fletcher turned it back to the buzz of notifications of voice mails. His pulse quickened with hope that one was from Kiki. He hadn't seen her since that night at the hospital. But that had been for her sake as much as his.

He didn't want his investigation to put her in danger again. But the only way to make sure she was really safe was to close the case. To find the Slasher.

He checked his voice mail and found two messages. One from the hospital in Conners and another from the medical examiner in San Francisco. He played the one from the hospital first. The doctor thought that Greg would be regaining consciousness soon.

And if that happened, Fletcher wanted to take his statement. If he could talk, that was. If he remembered anything after that blow he'd taken to his head and if he'd avoided the potential brain damage it may have caused.

But if he could talk, Fletcher wanted to know if the man had seen his assailant. Though, given what he'd discovered about Greg's trust, Fletcher wasn't all that certain that the Slasher had attacked Greg or someone else had.

He rushed off to Conners, but it was late when he arrived. This late at night, the ICU was relatively dark and, except for the beep of the machines monitoring the patients, mostly quiet. Visiting hours had ended long ago. Only doctors and nurses walked around the floor, and patients were monitored through the glass walls separating their rooms from the nurses' station. It must have been a shift change or something because nobody sat at the station now.

And when Fletcher glanced through the glass wall to Greg Stehouwer's room, he noticed a shadow looming over the bed, reminding him of how, just a couple of nights ago, he had found Troy looming over Kiki's bed.

But Troy had just been standing there.

This person clutched a pillow in their hands, and they pressed that pillow over the face of the patient lying in the bed. Over Greg Stehouwer.

Fletcher rushed into the room, locked his arms around the person and pulled them back. The person thrashed in his grasp, trying to break free. But Fletcher dragged the attacker to the floor, like he had with Troy that night. This time, at least, his arm was healing and the stitches didn't reopen like last time.

Troy was skinny and not very strong. But this guy fought back, throwing elbows, trying desperately to break free and escape.

"I'm Detective Colton. You're under arrest," Fletcher told the guy. "Stop resisting!"

An elbow landed in his ribs, knocking the breath from his lungs, and the guy surged to his feet. But Fletcher drew his weapon then. "I will shoot you!"

The guy froze, and light suddenly flooded the room, illuminating Greg's attacker. His brother. Gerard stood over Fletcher, his face flushed, his hair disheveled. He glanced at the nurse who'd entered the room. Her face was flushed, too. And the glance they exchanged...

"I'm Detective Colton," Fletcher said again. "Call security." He didn't trust her to do that, though, because it looked like she might be part of this. Had Gerard paid her to make sure that the nurses' station was empty when he'd attempted to end his brother's life? "No," he said when she started moving toward the doorway. "Stay here with your coconspirator." And he called Conners' police department for backup instead.

For the past couple of days, the houseboat had felt so empty without Fletcher that it was difficult for Kiki to stay there. And even harder to sleep.

But she didn't want to put her grandpa in danger, just in case Fletcher was right to be so worried about her safety. Although, if he was worried, why hadn't he checked on her? Why hadn't he called?

Or better yet, why hadn't he come home?

No. Not home. This wasn't his home. It wasn't hers either. She was just staying there while she was in Owl Creek and that was just for the rest of the summer.

Fletcher had sent that patrol car past the place several times. She'd seen it earlier that evening when she and Fancy had started out for their walk. Maybe a long walk in the night air would clear her head and hopefully her heart, too, because it was too full of feelings right now. Feelings she didn't want to have.

Kiki had taken such a long walk that both she and Fancy were worn out. All she wanted to do was go back to the boat and crawl into bed. But then she remembered that the sheets and pillows would smell like Fletcher. And she knew she would just lie there, yearning for him.

To be with him. To have his arms wrapped around her, holding her close like he had every night for the last several nights.

Her footsteps slowed on the dock as she neared the slip where the houseboat was anchored. She didn't want to be there without Fletcher.

Was it already too late? Had she already fallen for him?

It didn't matter how she felt if he didn't return her feelings. And even if he did, how in the world could a relationship between them last?

His life was here in Owl Creek. His job. His family.

She only had her grandfather here and some friends. But her life, her career, was taking her other places and probably always would.

"Ah, Fancy…" she murmured with a weary sigh.

The puppy whined and pulled at her leash, tugging Kiki toward the boat. Then Kiki looked up and saw what the puppy must have spotted. A light was on inside the cabin. A light that Kiki hadn't left on since it hadn't been dark out yet when she and Fancy had left earlier.

Since she hadn't left that light on, who had?

Fletcher?

Had he come back to the boat after all? Maybe she'd read him all wrong at the hospital the other night. Maybe he hadn't been trying to create distance between them the past couple of days; maybe he'd just been busy.

Eager to see him, she helped Fancy onto the boat deck and then jumped onto it herself. Fancy, her leash trailing behind her, rushed through the open door of the cabin. But instead of yipping with excitement, as she did every time she saw Fletcher, she growled instead.

And Kiki knew that it wasn't Fletcher who'd turned on that light but someone else. Someone Fancy instinctively didn't like or trust. And the little dog had very good instincts about people.

If Fancy didn't like or trust the person, Kiki shouldn't either. She should turn and run for help.

But she couldn't leave the little puppy alone on the boat with whoever was in the cabin making her growl like she was. Kiki couldn't let anything happen to the dog she was supposed to be fostering and protecting.

She just had to figure out, with her pepper spray gone, how she was going to protect them both.

Chapter 22

Fletcher was lead detective for a reason. He was good at breaking a suspect. And it had taken only a few minutes in the interrogation room for him to get the nurse to talk. She'd openly shared how Gerard had spent the past couple of weeks trying to charm her into doing what he wanted. Into killing his brother.

She'd refused to unplug his machine when he'd needed it to breathe. Or so she claimed.

But Fletcher intended to find out exactly how the doctors had realized Greg was able to breathe on his own. Maybe she *had* unplugged it. She was demanding immunity, though, to spill all on Gerard. So Fletcher encouraged her to talk some more.

And she'd admitted to making sure that he had a clear shot at his brother. That he'd intended to suffocate him and just make it look like he'd stopped breathing again.

Greg was still alive, though.

And Fletcher made sure his brother knew it when he walked into the interrogation room where he'd left him. He glanced around. "No lawyer? I thought you called your parents. Your wife…"

Nobody had retained a lawyer for him, probably not once they'd realized that he was going to be charged with the attempted murder of his own brother.

Gerard didn't say a word, just gritted his teeth as if it was a struggle to hold back what he really wanted to say. Maybe it wouldn't take Fletcher much longer to break him than it had the nurse.

"Your little friend had no problem talking to me," Fletcher shared. "She gave her statement about how you tried to hire her to kill your brother. You wanted her to finish the job you weren't able to do on your own."

The guy glared at him.

"So you're not what I expected the Slasher to be," he said. And he still wasn't. "But it's going to be good to charge you for all those crimes, too, in all those other states. Close all those cases. And you can pick what prison you'd like to spend the majority of your life in."

"I'm not the Slasher."

He wasn't. He had alibis for the other attacks. Fletcher had already checked that. "Those other precincts can't wait to close those cases—put the Slasher away for good."

"I'm not the Slasher," Gerard repeated.

"No, but you borrowed the Slasher's MO when you

tried to kill your brother in the parking lot of Club Ignition. And I know you're the one who did that, Gerard. The warehouse next to the club, the one nearest the parking lot, is in the process of being renovated, too. In order to protect the materials being delivered, they installed a security system."

Gerard shook his head. "That's not true."

No. It wasn't, but Fletcher needed his suspect to think it was.

"You would have said something sooner if you saw..." Gerard trailed off and swallowed deeply, nervously.

"If I saw you trying to kill your brother on camera," Fletcher finished for him. "We didn't know about that security footage until the other night, when there was another attack outside the club." He gestured at his bandaged arm. "It's all over now, Gerard."

Tears rolled down Gerard's face. "He doesn't deserve it. He doesn't deserve it," he murmured.

"No. He didn't deserve to be attacked like that," Fletcher agreed.

"No. Greg doesn't deserve the trust. He's only marrying Melanie so he can get his hands on our grandparents' money. He never visited them. He was never nice to them. Not like I was. He doesn't deserve it."

So, as Fletcher had suspected, it was all about money. "And if Greg is gone, the rest of that trust will go to you?"

Gerard nodded. "I deserve it. He doesn't. He doesn't deserve it."

Fletcher sighed and stood up, leaving the man to

cry alone in the interrogation room. He'd closed that case, but the Slasher's identity was still up in the air.

And that was the person Fletcher wanted to catch the most, especially since his arm was throbbing again. That dull ache kept reminding him of why he was staying away from Kiki—that it was to keep her safe.

But he missed her so damn much.

After stepping out of the interrogation room, he checked his phone again like he had earlier. But there were no new voice mails. Kiki hadn't called him.

He hadn't returned the medical examiner's call yet. But since it was earlier in San Francisco than it was in Owl Creek, he hit the button to call the ME back.

"Detective Colton returning your call," he said.

"Detective Colton," the doctor greeted him. "I'm glad you called back. I have some interesting information about Caitlin Sullivan."

"You found her?"

"I did, and her father knows it. He identified her body but refused to take it."

"What?"

"She had overdosed on drugs," the doctor said. "And he was furious about it. Said she got what she deserved and her dealer would be next."

Was that why the Slasher attacked those men? Did he think the men he'd targeted had been drug dealers? Was that the motivation for all those attacks?

Kiki rushed into the cabin after Fancy, trying to catch her leash, trying to pull her away from the man kicking out at her as the puppy tugged on the already frayed legs of Troy's tattered jeans. "Come!" she commanded the dog. She just managed to catch her leash as she moved to make the hand gesture. She didn't want Fancy anywhere near Troy.

She didn't want Troy anywhere near her. Wasn't he supposed to be in the hospital? Or jail? Fletcher had been determined to arrest him.

"What are you doing here?" she asked as she held tightly to the leash. Fancy struggled to get to Troy who sat on the couch where she'd found him the last time he'd broken in.

There was no broken glass this time. Not since she'd fixed the door. But she must have left it unlocked. Maybe she'd done that in the hopes that Fletcher would show up.

She wished he was here now.

"I wanted to talk to you, Kiki," he said. "To say I'm sorry…"

She was, too. So sorry that she hadn't checked him out more thoroughly before she'd asked him to help her. "No. I mean… Why are you here? And not in the hospital or…"

"Jail?" he asked. "Your old friend arrested and interrogated me."

"And let you go?" Fletcher wouldn't have done that if he still suspected Troy was the Slasher.

His usually pale face flushed in the glow of the lamp that he'd turned on next to the couch. "He didn't let me go. But I got bail."

"And you had the money for that?" But not to pay his child support?

"I—I thought you paid it," he said.

She stared at him in disbelief. "Really? Why?"

"I—I thought we were friends, Kiki," he said. "We've known each other so long."

"I don't know if I ever really knew you," she said. And she didn't want to get to know him. "I had no idea about the drugs, Troy."

"I'm going to get clean," he said. "I'm going to go to rehab."

"And your kids?" she asked. "How could you just abandon them? Stop supporting them?"

"I-it's more complicated than that, Kiki," he said. "There's more to the story. I'm no good for them. Not now. But maybe after rehab…"

"I hope you go," she said.

"I already signed up at the hospital," Troy said. "A doctor got me a room at a place. I can go now that I got out of jail. That's why I thought you paid the bail. I thought…"

She shook her head. "It wasn't me, Troy. I want you to go to rehab. But I really just want you to leave. And please, don't come back again."

She didn't think he would have been given bail if he'd actually been charged with the attacks the Slasher had committed. But it didn't matter to her. She didn't want to deal with Troy anymore.

"Kiki, I'm really sorry," he said.

"I'm sorry, too," a deep voice said from behind Kiki. And she whirled around as Fancy snapped and snarled at the man who'd snuck up on them both.

"Mr. Sullivan?" she asked, staring at him in shock.

"What—what are you doing here?" And why had he apologized to her?

Troy's face paled again until he looked like death, and he stared at Mr. Sullivan in shock. "It was you," he murmured. "It was you."

"What was him?" Kiki asked. The Slasher? Was Mr. Sullivan the Slasher? He stood between her and the door, and she didn't know how she would get away from him, especially if he had that knife she'd seen in the alley. That long, sharp machete that had cut through the air and slashed Fletcher's arm.

She should have checked on him and made sure that he was okay. That his wound had healed.

Regret weighed heavily on her for so many things. Fletcher. And not replacing her empty canister of pepper spray. She had a feeling that she was going to need it now.

"I bailed Troy out," Mr. Sullivan said.

"Why—why would you do that?" Kiki asked. "I didn't even know you knew each other."

"We don't," Troy said. "I've just seen him around the clubs when he's been looking for his daughter."

Mr. Sullivan shook his head. "I know where she is. Thanks to you, Troy. You're the one I've been looking for. I didn't know it was you until Bart told me, but now I know you're the one who got my little girl hooked on drugs."

Troy shook his head. "No, no. Not me."

"You don't deal drugs out of the clubs?" Dan Sullivan snorted. "Don't lie to me."

Troy's pale face flushed again. "I—I might have

from time to time when I needed money. And people needed something to feel good."

Dan's face flushed now. "Caitlin didn't need to feel good. She needed to grow up. To deal with life like an adult instead of running away and hiding from her problems like a child. Like you've been running away and hiding, Troy. It's time to face the consequences of your bad choices now, just like Caitlin faced her consequences."

Kiki tensed. He'd always acted like such a distraught father. "You knew where she's been all this time?" she asked with surprise. "You knew she was dead."

"Caitlin paid for her mistakes," Dan said. "Now it's time for Troy to pay for his."

"What about me?" Kiki asked. "I didn't know what he was doing."

Dan snorted. "Really? You worked with him for how long and had no idea what he was doing?"

She shook her head. "I really, really didn't know." But she doubted that was going to matter to Dan Sullivan. Because she saw now what he'd been holding behind his back...

It wasn't a knife like the one the Slasher had used in the alley. This was a gun, which was even more dangerous. He wouldn't even have to get close to them to kill them. And she had no doubt that was what he intended to do, or he wouldn't have brought the weapon with him.

"Then I really, really am sorry," Dan said.

Troy shook his head. "C'mon, man, she's not part of this," he said. "Let her go."

"What? So she can get help for you? Like that rehab you think you're getting into?" Dan shook his head. "I can't have that. I can't have you getting better, getting your life back when you took mine."

"I didn't have anything to do with this," Kiki said. "So if you kill me, that's going to make you as bad as you think Troy is. Actually, worse. He didn't know that your daughter was going to die." And Dan had every intention of killing her.

And Kiki had every intention of making sure that didn't happen. She wasn't going to die like this. But she wasn't sure how to stop Dan from shooting her and Troy.

Chapter 23

Fletcher had intended to talk to Troy again about Dan Sullivan. But when he went to see him in the cells, he found that he'd been bailed out. And when he found out who had bailed him out...

"Dan Sullivan," Fletcher murmured. "Why in the hell would he have bailed out a drug user like Troy?" But then he knew why.

For revenge.

Troy could be more than a drug user. He could be a dealer as well. He'd mentioned something about rehab during their interview earlier. But a call to his doctor confirmed he hadn't checked in yet. So where would he have gone?

Security footage from the jail showed him walking out on his own. Nobody had picked him up. He'd just walked off. The marina wasn't far from the police department. Every other time he'd come around town, Troy had sought out Kiki. Fletcher figured the man was in love with her. He understood all too well how easy it would be to fall for her, especially after watching her DJ, after hearing her sing and seeing her dance and how the music flowed through her like joy.

And how that joy flowed over onto everyone around her.

Troy might not have been the only one who fell for Kiki. Fletcher didn't think Dan Sullivan had, though, so he probably wouldn't care if Kiki wound up as collateral damage in his quest for revenge.

Fletcher jumped in his Owl Creek PD vehicle, but he didn't engage the lights and sirens. He didn't want to alert anyone that he was coming. Except Kiki.

He hoped she knew if she was in danger that he would rush to her rescue like she'd rushed to his. But he had to make sure that he could actually rescue her and that he wasn't already too late.

Once he parked his SUV, he hurried along the dock, but this time he was careful to keep his footsteps as quiet as he could. He didn't want anyone to hear him coming and he kept to the shadows the boats cast on the dock despite the brightness of the full moon. But as he neared the boat, he knew someone had noticed him.

Kiki and Troy stood on the rear deck, near the railing, with Dan in front of them, his back toward the dock, toward Fletcher. Fancy stood next to Kiki, quivering and snarling with fear and anger.

She knew the man was a threat even if she didn't understand that he was holding a gun. The barrel pointed directly at Kiki's big heart. Fancy was the one who saw him, and she started yipping until he held up a hand the way that Kiki had taught him. The hold command.

Stay.

Don't Move.

Don't React.

He silently told her all those things, and somehow the puppy must have understood his commands because she stayed next to Kiki and she stayed quiet, barely betraying any interest in him. So he was able to creep closer.

But if he jumped on the boat, it might shift beneath his weight and reveal his presence. He hadn't ever seen anyone on the boat docked next to hers when he'd stayed with Kiki. He could probably get on it without bothering whoever the owner was. But if he stepped onto it, would it shift enough in the water to move her boat, too?

From where he was, he couldn't get a clear shot at Sullivan. The cabin blocked most of his body, leaving just his hand and that gun most visible to Fletcher. Fletcher was a good shot, but hitting a hand wasn't easy.

And if the man pulled the trigger convulsively, he was going to put a bullet right into Kiki's heart. And that was like putting a bullet in Fletcher's, too. He couldn't lose her. Not like this…

Fletcher was there. Kiki knew it from the way that Fancy's tail had wagged and the way that she'd whined. Kiki couldn't see him, but it was enough that Fancy had, enough that she'd minded the command he'd given her.

Wait.

Stay.

Kiki had to tell herself to do the same thing. She had to stall for more time, like she had earlier, when she'd convinced Dan not to shoot them within the cabin but to come up to the deck.

To make them jump into the water with the anchor tied around their feet.

"People will hear the gunshot," she'd told him. "I'm not the only one living on their boat. Other people will see you, will stop you. You won't get away."

She wasn't sure that he'd wanted to, though. Maybe, because his daughter was dead, he intended to kill himself once he'd killed her dealer.

And Kiki.

But clearly, he wasn't done yet. "I have to kill Bart, too," he told them as he pushed them closer to the railing behind them. "I know he's part of this." He pointed the gun at Troy. "He works with you, with the drugs."

Troy let out a shaky breath. "He didn't have anything to do with your daughter, sir. I don't think I did either. I didn't recognize her picture when you showed me. I don't think I knew her."

"You sold to her," Dan insisted, waving his gun in a hand that shook with his fury.

As upset as he was, he might accidentally pull that trigger. She tried to ease between him and Troy. He might be less likely to pull the trigger and kill her since he knew for certain that she had nothing to do with his daughter's death.

"There are a lot of dealers in the clubs," Troy insisted. "Customers. Bouncers."

"Bartenders and you," Dan said. "I know you and Bart work together. That's why I paid him to get you into the club. I was going to kill you by cutting you up like that maniac cuts up his victims in the alley." He focused on Kiki again. "But you brought that cop into the place."

So much for Fletcher's cover.

She didn't want to lie to Sullivan and set him off any more than he already was. Because she'd felt that faint motion as the boat moved in the water. Either someone had stepped onto it or onto the boat next to it, causing a ripple along the surface of the water. "He is a cop," she admitted. "He was going undercover to catch the Slasher. How did you know that?"

Dan pointed his gun at Troy again. "He told Bart. He saw you both outside his van that first night, saw that he drove a police vehicle."

And so, Troy had given him up, maybe warning Bart to lie low with the drug dealing while Fletcher was there.

"Not all clubgoers are that bad," Kiki said in defense of her job. "Some people are just there to dance, to enjoy the music, to meet other people."

Dan snorted. "You're naive, Kiki."

"No, I see the good in people. I don't think the worst of everyone I meet."

"That's why you're here," he said. "With an anchor tied around your ankles."

She'd done the tying. It was about as tight as Fletcher

laced his boots now. She would be able to get it off, and so would Troy if he didn't panic. He was panicking now, his body shaking, his breath coming in pants that were getting higher and shallower, like he was about to hyperventilate.

If he went into the water like that, he was going to drown before they ever got the rope and anchor off. She had to keep stalling to give Fletcher time to rescue them. But would he rescue them or put himself in more danger, like he had the night he'd gone into that alley looking for her?

"It's time now," Sullivan said. "Enough stalling. Time for the two of you to jump over the railing. Time to end this."

Troy started crying now. Soft, gasping sobs. And tears rolled down his face.

Instead of being moved, Dan Sullivan laughed. "You're not making me feel sorry for you. Not at all." He looked at Kiki and his mouth slid into a frown. "You, I feel sorry for—having to die with a scumbag like him. It would be better for you to die alone."

Even if Dan and Troy weren't there, she wouldn't have died alone. Fletcher was there. She could see him now inside the cabin of her boat, moving toward them. Fancy saw him, too, and whined deep in her throat, as if anxious to rush toward him, to leap and lick all over him like she usually did.

Kiki wanted to do the same, but she was too scared. For her and Troy and for Fletcher, too.

Dan had to think he was in charge. He seemed like a man who was always in control. Could that be why his daughter had rebelled with the clubbing and the drugs? Maybe he'd been too controlling.

Instead of crying, Kiki shook her head as if she pitied him. "This is sad."

"What do you mean?" he asked.

"That you're not strong enough to deal with your grief and your regrets about your daughter," she said.

He bristled and tightened his grasp on the gun. "You don't know what you're talking about!"

"I lost my parents," she said. "In a traffic accident. I didn't blame the other driver even though he left the scene. I didn't have to chase him down and avenge my parents."

"You must have been a kid when that happened," Dan guessed. Correctly. "And you would have felt better if you had."

"I felt better letting them go with grace and with honoring their memories by being the best person I could be," she said. "I didn't become bitter and crazy. I didn't lose control so badly that I turned into a monster."

"Shut up!" Dan yelled at her. "You don't know what you're talking about! Shut up!" And he swung that barrel back from Troy to her, focusing it on her heart. And his finger moved toward the trigger.

Troy stopped crying to gasp and he even pointed at Fletcher, tipping Dan off to him sneaking onto the boat. Kiki reached out, trying to lower his arm, trying to get him to stop. And Troy toppled back, falling over the railing. The rope wound through the anchor and lashed around both of their ankles. If Troy was heavy enough, he might pull that anchor over with him, and then Kiki would go into the water, too.

But she cared less about that than about Fletcher as Dan spun around toward the cabin, his gun raised and his finger moving toward the trigger, squeezing and firing off a bullet in Fletcher's direction.

Fletcher's gun was out, too, but he might not fire back, might worry about hitting her and Troy with the way they were behind Dan. But then they weren't there as Troy fell into the water, taking a piece of the deck railing with him as the anchor struck it, breaking it.

And that rope tightened around Kiki's ankles, pulling her off the boat and into the water, too. And then down into the depths of the lake.

She was worried about herself and Troy, but she was the most worried about Fletcher. She had a chance to loosen that rope again, to free herself and Troy from the anchor.

But if Fletcher had been shot…

Chapter 24

The first bullet missed Fletcher. The second was never fired because Fletcher didn't miss. He dropped Dan Sullivan to the deck. And then he went over the railing after Kiki and Troy. She broke through the water, coming up as he sank down into the lake.

She tossed her head, sending water spraying, and then she started slipping under again. And Fletcher could see Troy pulling her down as he flailed and panicked.

Fletcher swam to him, trying to break his grasp on Kiki. But he kept pulling at her, pinching her skin, pulling her under the water. So Fletcher swung his fist, knocking the guy out. And then he carried him up as Kiki shot back to the surface.

Sirens whined in the distance. Fletcher had sent out a text to dispatch. They'd been on their way with the order to come in stealthily. Maybe a report of shots fired had had them turning on the sirens and lights.

Backup arrived too late to save Dan Sullivan. But it had probably been too late to save him long before Fletcher shot him. He didn't know if the same was true about Troy, but instead of going to the hospital, he'd wanted to go to that rehab program. So after giving his statement for the police report, he was given a ride to the facility. Officer Blaine was to make sure that he really checked in, because Fletcher still had his doubts about the man.

Fletcher still had a lot of doubts about a lot of parts of this case. And even about Kiki.

Fletcher had wanted Kiki to go to the hospital, too, but she'd insisted she was fine. He wasn't so sure that she was because she kept trembling even though the water hadn't been cold. And thanks to how loosely she'd tied the anchor rope to her and to Troy, neither of them had been under water for very long.

Fletcher wasn't fine. Physically there wasn't anything wrong with him. He hadn't reopened the stitches on his arm. But emotionally…

He was as on edge as he'd been when he'd seen Sullivan pointing that gun barrel at Kiki's heart. Even after they finished giving their statements to police and everyone had left, he was still jumpy. Maybe more so because it was just the two of them. And Fancy, who'd curled up at his feet as he sat on the deck, watching the sun come up.

Kiki had gone inside to change out of her wet shorts and shirt. And clearly when she walked back out, drying her hair on a towel, she hadn't expected to see him still there. Her dark eyes widened in surprise. And he couldn't tell if she was happy or upset that he hadn't left.

Then those eyes suddenly welled with tears that sparkled in the light. And Fletcher jumped up and rushed to her, closing his arms around her.

Kiki, being Kiki, didn't cry. She didn't give in to tears, but she closed her arms around him and clutched him close. And they just held each other.

He was alive. When she'd gone over the side, she hadn't known what she would find when she resurfaced. Fletcher dead? The thought had horrified her, making her move even faster to ease out of the rope and fight her way out of the water. She'd helped Troy, too, but in his panic, he might have drowned them both. If not for Fletcher jumping in after them...

Kiki and Troy were probably alive because of Fletcher. So maybe it was just gratitude that had her clinging to him like she was.

Or relief that they were all alive.

Well, not all of them.

Dan Sullivan hadn't made it. But she suspected he'd been gone a long time ago—lost to his hatred and bitterness and madness.

She was just glad she hadn't lost Fletcher. Yet.

She knew he was slipping away from her though. That their time together was coming to an end. They had no future. His life, his career, his family, were all here in Owl Creek.

He released a shaky breath that stirred her hair and

made her shiver. "I'm so glad you're all right." But then he pulled back and cupped her face in his hands, and he stared into her eyes with that intense stare that unnerved and excited her so damn much. "Are you really all right?"

She nodded and released a shaky breath of her own. For the moment, with him here, holding her, she was all right.

"I'm not," he said.

She could feel his body shaking against hers now. "Fletcher…"

"I was so scared when I saw him pointing that gun at you, so worried that it might accidentally go off and hurt you or…" He shuddered again.

And she closed her arms around him, then tugged him inside with her, through the open door to the cabin and then through the cabin to her bedroom.

Fancy was on their heels. But Kiki shut the little puppy out. Instead of whining, the exhausted dog just leaned against the door. She wanted to know that they were close.

That was what Kiki wanted, too. Just to have Fletcher close even if it was only for a little while longer.

"Kiki…" he murmured, and then he lowered his head to hers. At first his lips just brushed across hers in a gentle, almost reverent kiss.

Then she reached up and tangled her fingers in his damp hair, and she held his head against hers as she deepened the kiss. She teased him with her tongue.

His breath caught and then he kissed her back just

as passionately, just as desperately as she was kissing him. "Kiki..."

"We need to get you out of these wet clothes," she said, as she tugged his damp T-shirt over his head.

He shucked off his jeans and boxers and stood before her, gloriously naked. He was so perfect. His chest and thighs so muscular. His stomach so lean.

She lifted the T-shirt dress she'd pulled on to replace her wet clothes. And his breath shuddered out in a ragged groan.

"You are so beautiful," he said. His fingers, shaking slightly, traced her every curve with the reverence that had been in his first kiss. Then his lips replaced his fingers.

He kissed her everywhere, and passion overwhelmed her, making her legs shake. She tumbled back onto the bed, pulling him with her. She loved the weight of him, the heat of him, on top of her. His heart beat in time with hers, fast and furiously.

"Fletcher, I need you," she admitted. She felt a flicker of unease as she said it, concerned that she wasn't talking about just now, but forever.

But she'd never needed anyone like that.

Instead of joining their bodies like she needed him to do, he moved down hers. He kissed her breasts, flicking his tongue across each nipple, and then he moved lower, making love to her with his mouth.

She clutched the sheets as the pressure built inside her and then released in an orgasm that left her shuddering and gasping for breath. She closed her eyes, riding the peak of pleasure. And she heard a cupboard open, a packet tear and then he eased inside her, stretching her, filling her completing her.

He began to move, building that tension again. She clutched at him, locking her legs around him, grabbing his shoulders. She met his thrusts, arching up, holding him close, pulling him deeper.

He groaned. And his mouth covered hers, kissing her, imitating with his tongue what he was doing with his body. And that pressure inside her burst again, filling her with pleasure.

Then his body tensed. A deep groan slipped between his lips as he found his release. He flopped onto his back, carrying her with him so that she was on top and their bodies were still joined. And he stared up into her face with such an expression...

Of awe and wonder.

It probably mirrored the expression on her face.

"You are amazing," he whispered. Then he arched up and kissed her, and it was that soft tender kiss that had her heart swelling and warming.

And...

No. She could not fall for Fletcher, but she had a feeling that it was already too late.

They made love again. More slowly, more reverently, before finally settling onto the bed to rest sometime later. But Kiki couldn't sleep. And his body was tense beside hers despite all the orgasms they'd had.

"Why did you come here?" she asked. She hoped it was because he'd missed her like she'd missed him.

"I found out that Dan Sullivan's daughter was dead

and that he refused to claim her body. It also sounded like he was going after her drug dealer."

"Troy."

"And when he bailed him out, I figured he was going to go after him, wherever he was."

So he hadn't come to see her. He hadn't missed her the past couple of days like she'd missed him.

"And I figured, knowing how he kept turning up wherever you were, that Troy might be here, putting you in danger and…" His gruff voice trailed off and he shuddered and pulled her closer. "I was so worried that I would be too late."

"You were right on time," she said with a slight smile. Then she asked, "Is it over?" And she wasn't really asking about the case. She wondered about the two of them…

"I don't think Dan Sullivan or Gerard Stehouwer are the Slasher," he said.

"Gerard Stehouwer?"

"Greg's brother is the one who tried to kill him. Twice, actually. Once in the parking lot and once in the ICU."

She had a feeling that Fletcher had stopped that from happening, just as he'd stopped Dan Sullivan from killing Troy. "Then who is the Slasher?" she asked. "Do you still suspect Troy?"

"I don't know. I have the note the Slasher slipped me. There is some DNA on it. We'll see if it matches Troy's or Gerard's or Dan's."

"And if it doesn't?"

"Then the Slasher is still out there." He tightened his arms around her. "But I will catch whoever it is, Kiki."

At what cost, she wondered. His life? Her heart? She had a feeling they were both in danger.

According to the latest media reports, the stupid people of Owl Creek believed that the Slasher was either dead or in jail. That the grief-stricken old man or the rich frat boy was the Slasher. The Slasher hated this, hated how other people hadn't just copycatted but tried to pretend to be the Slasher.

That wasn't admiration. That was disrespect.

And the Slasher had already been disrespected enough. It was time to end this once and for all.

Chapter 25

Fletcher knew it was a risk coming back to Club Ignition with Kiki. It was a risk to him because the more time he spent with her, the more he was falling for her. And she wasn't going to stay. As she played and sang and danced, he could see the star that she was, burning much too bright for Owl Creek.

He didn't want to hold her back. But he was so damn tempted to try. But that would have been selfish. And he cared about her too much to be that way with her.

"You know your cover is blown," Bart told him as he poured a cup of coffee for Fletcher and pushed it across the bar.

Fletcher had brought his own thermos, like Kiki brought her tea. He wasn't taking any chances anymore. At least not with his life.

With his heart.

He took a chance every time he was around Kiki.

Fletcher chuckled. "I really am an old friend of Kiki's," he said. "And I really am her assistant." But he wanted to be so much more.

Bart snorted and shook his head. "Okay, sure, but you're still a cop, too."

"Lead detective," Fletcher said with pride in the title. Now if only he could live up to it...

His new boss was happy with him for closing a couple of big cases. Greg Stehouwer's attack. And Dan Sullivan's attempted crimes.

His boss thought Fletcher had closed the Slasher case, too. But Fletcher didn't think so.

The Slasher was still out there. Maybe even here tonight now that Club Ignition had reopened.

"Did you get promoted after closing the Slasher case?" Bart asked.

"It's not closed," Fletcher said. At least not as far as he was concerned.

"So that's why you're back here."

"I'm just helping out Kiki until she can find a new assistant."

"I thought Troy was getting clean," Bart said. "That he went into rehab."

"That doesn't mean Kiki will work with him again." Fletcher studied Bart's face. "Sullivan said you worked with Troy selling drugs. He was coming for you next."

"I guess I owe you a thank you then," Bart said. "You made sure that bitter old man won't hurt anyone else.

And he was wrong about me. I'm not selling anything but drinks."

Fletcher pushed the coffee mug across the bar toward Bart. "I was drugged that night that Kiki and I were attacked in the alley."

"Then I guess you should have kept a better eye on your cup," Bart said. "Because I didn't put anything in it."

"The other victims had been drugged, too," Fletcher said.

"It wasn't me," Bart said. "I'm not a drug user. And I am damn well not that violent Slasher. Anybody can get close enough to drop something in someone else's glass."

And a note in their pocket?

Fletcher might have believed that Bart had drugged the drinks, but he wouldn't have been able to slip him a note, not when he rarely left his place behind the bar.

"You're the detective," Bart said. "So you must have thought about how a lot of these were at bachelor parties. They usually do shots, line them up at the bar, but a lot of people buy the groom drinks, too. A lot of women."

"Women..." The DNA on that note had recently come back as not a match to Dan Sullivan or Gerard Stehouwer because it had belonged to a woman. An unidentified woman.

Fletcher's boss hadn't considered it that much of a lead. And Fletcher had agreed because the Slasher had never left any DNA behind at any other scene, so he would have made certain not to leave any on the note either. They'd assumed that the woman must have just touched the paper at some point.

Bart's head bobbed in a nod. "Yeah, it's not just guys buying girls drinks anymore. You know, women's lib. A lot of women buy drinks for men, too."

The Slasher was a woman. It made total sense. It was how she was able to get so close to shove a note in the guy's pocket. And how, even though that knife was sharp, the wound on Fletcher's arm hadn't been deeper.

The Slasher was a woman, but which woman? Was she here tonight?

The club was packed. Probably because the news had all made it sound like the Slasher had either been arrested or killed. But Kiki knew that wasn't the case. The DNA results on that note shoved in Fletcher's pocket hadn't matched Dan Sullivan or Gerard Stehouwer's. It had belonged to a woman.

Fletcher hadn't been as quick to accept that, though, pointing out how the Slasher had never left any DNA behind before and probably would have made certain to leave none on the note.

Sure, no DNA had been left at the scene of the crimes because the Slasher wore that hazmat-type suit. Ones that had been all too available during the pandemic. But the Slasher wouldn't have been able to wear that suit inside the club without being noticed, especially when slipping a note into the pocket of their chosen victim.

The Slasher had chosen Fletcher once. Had slipped Fletcher that note.

It had to be a woman. And Kiki remembered who'd

been dancing so closely to him when he'd started acting so out of it.

Her girls. Amy, Claire and Janie.

She hadn't seen any of them when she'd gone looking for him. Of course, she hadn't looked for him in the ladies' room, so they'd probably been in there.

Or…

Maybe one of them had been in the alley, waiting for him to come out that door. Waiting to attack him.

She shuddered as she remembered that night, how close she'd come to losing him. And the turntable skipped a beat. She steadied her hand and kept spinning while her thoughts spun as well.

She and Fletcher had both been scared about coming back to the club, but they'd each been frightened for the other. She'd promised she would stay inside her booth, and he'd promised he wouldn't drink anything but the coffee that was in the thermos next to hers. And he wouldn't go out into the alley without backup.

An officer from Conners was here tonight, blending in with the crowd. There was another bachelor party here; maybe they thought it was safe, though.

That the Slasher was gone.

But Kiki saw her girls jumping up and down in the crowd. They weren't all dancing together; they'd joined that group from the bachelor party. Some of the guys were grinding up on them. Some of the women were returning the favor.

And then she noticed the slip of paper in Janie's hand, how the strobe light flashed against the white material and bounced back at her.

How had Kiki never noticed that before?

Because she hadn't been looking for it.

Then the paper disappeared. And then Janie did as well, disappearing into the crowd. Had she slipped that paper into a man's pocket?

And which man?

Kiki called out, "Where's my assistant at?" Then making her voice sound like Lucille Ball's, she said, "Fletcher, I need you."

The crowd laughed at her impression. But she didn't see Fletcher among them. Where had he gone? Was he already in the alley? If he was, he was in danger.

Because Kiki was pretty sure the Slasher was heading out there now.

The machete was sharper than it had ever been, the blade honed so that it would slice through skin and maybe even bone now. If Janie could swing it hard enough...

And she was damn sure that she would.

She wasn't just going to maim this idiot. She was going to kill him.

Maybe that was what it was going to take for her to finally get the respect she deserved. The respect her ex-fiancé hadn't given her.

He'd called her stupid and ugly and so far beneath him that he'd been a fool to ever propose to her. He hadn't been a fool when Janie had paid his way through med school.

No. She had been his everything then. He'd showered

her with compliments and gratitude even as he'd kept putting off their wedding day.

And even though he hadn't been home much, she'd believed it was just because of his long hours. Especially during his residency.

Residents didn't make any real money, he told her, so they would get married after he became an attending physician. Then he would be making so much money that they could have the wedding of their dreams. The wedding she deserved to have for everything she'd done for him.

But once he'd gotten his job offer and his six-figure salary, he'd asked for his ring back. He'd never intended to marry someone like her. As a rich doctor, he could do so much better than her.

Once Janie had taken care of his face, his new fiancée had thought she could do better, too, and she'd dumped him just like he had dumped Janie.

But that hadn't been enough for her. Because when she'd gone out to the club, she'd seen all those other grooms-to-be flirting with women, eager to cheat on their fiancées. Janie had decided that they didn't deserve their brides. They didn't deserve their happiness, and she'd taken it away from them.

She wanted to take away more than someone's happiness tonight. She intended to take away his life. And Kiki wasn't going to stop her this time.

Chapter 26

Fletcher had the note. *Meet me in the alley and I will show you a good time...*

It wasn't his. He'd taken it off the man who'd stumbled through the kitchen, intent on going out to the alley to meet the woman who had slipped him the note on the dance floor.

The Slasher wasn't going to get the hapless groom-to-be that she'd tried to lure outside. She was going to get Fletcher. He drew his weapon from his holster and pushed open the door to the alley. The metal hinges creaked, announcing his arrival. But nothing moved in the shadows.

Was the Slasher out there?

Or had this been a distraction? An attempt to get Fletcher's attention somewhere else while she attacked...

Kiki?

No. Kiki was safe. Someone had actually helped him out with that, jamming the door to the DJ booth so that Kiki hadn't been able to get it open. She could have jumped over, like he regularly did. But he'd planted an officer in plainclothes next to it to keep Kiki safe.

What about him?

Was he safe?

He started down the wooden steps that led from the door to the asphalt of the alley. And he made sure to clomp his boots and shuffle, so he sounded like he was drunk.

Or drugged.

Fletcher would have him tested to determine what exactly was wrong with the man besides poor judgement. Fletcher's judgement might have been a little poor to walk out here on his own, especially after he made that promise to Kiki that he wouldn't.

But he wasn't alone. As he hit the bottom step and made certain to bang his shoulder, loudly, against the dumpster, the Slasher jumped out from the other side, brandishing that sharp weapon.

But he had his gun trained on her, and then lights flooded the alley and other officers jumped from their hiding place inside the abandoned warehouse on the other side of the alley.

The Slasher held tight to the hilt of the knife, though, as if tempted to swing it. To try to kill him.

"Drop it, Janie," he said. The groom-to-be had told him that the redhead must have given him the note, that she'd been dancing closest to him. "Or I will kill you."

Finally, the knife dropped, clattering against the asphalt. And Janie dragged off the hood and mask and gasped for breath. "I hate you! I hate you! You can't stop me. You can't stop me now."

"It's over, Janie," he said. "You're under arrest."

"But it's not my fault," she said. "They don't have to cheat. They want to. And I want to make sure nobody ever wants them again."

He could imagine what her motivation was. "Jilted bride?" he asked.

"I hate you!" she screamed, and she bent down to grab the knife. But the other officers were there, grabbing her arms, pulling them behind her back to cuff her. "I hate you!"

He didn't doubt it. She was obviously full of hate right now. Just like Dan Sullivan had been.

And he thought of what Kiki had said to the man, about how she'd chosen forgiveness. How she hadn't wanted the bitterness and hatred to consume her. She'd chosen to live with happiness instead.

Just thinking of her, how incredible she was, made him smile.

"I hate you!" Janie raged as the officer struggled to lead her from the alley to where a patrol car waited to bring her to jail. She wouldn't get bail. Maybe a psychiatric evaluation, but not bail.

"I'll meet you at the station," he called out to his officers. He had to collect that groom-to-be and make sure his blood got tested and his official statement taken. But when he opened the door to step back into the kitchen, it wasn't him he found.

Kiki stood near the dishwasher with the officer at her

side, and she was shaking. "You promised!" she yelled at him. "You said you wouldn't go out there!"

"I wasn't alone," he said. "I had officers hiding out in the other building. We got her."

"Janie?" she asked.

He shouldn't have been surprised that she'd figured it out. She was as smart as she was beautiful. He nodded. "We got her. It's all over now."

She nodded now. "Yes, it is." Then she turned and walked away.

And he couldn't help but think she was talking about more than his case. About more than the Slasher, that she was talking about them as well.

And he was more scared than he'd been when he'd walked into that alley, uncertain of when and where the Slasher would come at him. At the moment, Kiki scared him more than he'd ever been scared because he didn't want them to be over. Now or ever.

Fletcher had scared her again, like that night he'd gone into the alley in place of the Slasher's chosen victim. The thought of losing him like she'd lost her parents had devastated her. She'd come so close so many times.

Thank goodness the Slasher had finally been caught. Janie.

There would be other dangerous cases for him. Other chances for her to lose him. And she'd thought that would be unbearable—more than she could survive because she'd also realized, during all those moments when she could have lost him, how much she wanted and loved him. Too much.

He'd stayed away from her the past week. Maybe he'd been busy wrapping up all the cases he'd closed. Or maybe he'd taken what she'd said in the heat of the moment at face value and believed she didn't want anything to do with him anymore, as her undercover assistant or as her lover.

But because he'd stayed away from her, Kiki had felt like she lost him already. During that week she'd slept very little, missing him too much, but she'd written and, in her songs, she'd found clarity. That there were no guarantees, but that love was worth the risk of loss. And that if it was meant to be, if they were meant to be, that they would figure out a way to be together and to be happy.

But she knew she wouldn't be happy, truly happy, if they weren't together. "Okay, Fancy," she told the puppy, who'd been moping as much as she'd been with missing Fletcher. "We're going to go get him back." This time she had a shirt in a gift bag. A pink and blue flannel one to replace the one that he'd claimed to hate. The Slasher had ruined it that first time she'd gone after Fletcher.

Janie.

Kiki still struggled to understand why, even though she'd talked to Claire and Amy and found out more about Janie. They hadn't been as close to her as she'd made it seem, but they'd known about her broken engagement. They swore they hadn't known that she was the Slasher. She believed them.

Jenny Colton was probably going to believe she was a stalker when Kiki showed up with another gift for her son. But before she could leave the boat, it shifted beneath the weight of someone jumping onto it.

She turned toward the door and saw Fletcher coming across the front deck toward her.

Fancy jumped up and yipped her happiness. While Kiki was excited, too, she contained herself. He'd stayed away for a week. Maybe he'd figured they were over, too. Whatever they were.

She wasn't even sure. They'd never put a label on what they had. What had her grandpa called it? Something-something...

It burned between them now as he stared at her. She wore a dress today—just a simple sleeveless, button-down denim one. He wore jeans and a T-shirt, like he was dressed to go undercover with her again.

But of course, it was Saturday, so he probably wasn't working today. He also carried a bag in his hand. One from a pet store.

"Hi," he said.

"Hi."

He pointed toward the bag that dangled from her fingers. "Were you going somewhere?" he asked.

She nodded. "Your house."

"My mom's?"

She nodded again.

"I don't live there anymore."

"You don't?" she asked, and nerves gripped her. "Are you leaving Owl Creek?"

He shook his head. "No. I bought a house of my own. Close to the police department and Frannie's bookstore. It has a nice, fenced yard that would be perfect for Fancy."

"You bought a house for Fancy?"

"I'm going to see if Sebastian and Ruby will let me adopt her," he said. "They can still train her and use her as a scent dog. But when she's not working, she can stay with me."

She narrowed her eyes and studied his face. That look was in his vivid green eyes, that intense look that always unsettled her. But this time it had the opposite effect. Her nerves settled and she smiled. "So that gift bag you brought is for her?"

He nodded and pulled out a chew toy. "Figured she might leave my boots and shoes alone if she had this instead." The puppy took the toy from him and dropped onto the floor to gnaw away at it.

"What about you?" he asked. "What's in your bag?"

She pulled out the flannel shirt. "I felt like I needed to replace this. I know how much you love it."

"I really do love it," he said. But he was staring at her, not the shirt. Then he stepped closer to her, until his body just about brushed up against hers.

"You must be relieved this case is over," she said. "You can go to bed early, sleep late… No more loud music or crowds."

"I actually miss it," he said.

"Liar."

"I miss you. And you know you can come to my house and visit Fancy anytime you're in town," he said.

She smiled. "That's generous of you. To let me visit the dog I've been fostering…"

"In addition to that fenced yard, it also has this special sound room in the basement. Former owner was a musician. You might like that."

"I might," she said.

"You can use that whenever you want," he said. "And you can stay however long you want, between gigs, you know…like…forever…"

Kiki's smile widened as joy filled her heart. "Sounds good to me."

"What part? The sound room? The fenced yard?" he asked.

"The forever." And she pulled his head down to hers, kissing him with all the love she felt for him. And all the passion.

The passion swept her up as Fletcher lifted and carried her into her bedroom. He kept his mouth on hers, kissing her deeply as he lowered her onto the bed. Then his fingers were on the buttons on her dress, undoing them all until the material fell away from her body, revealing her lacy bra and underwear. He unclasped the bra and hooked a finger in her underwear, pulling it down until she was completely bare.

And that look was in his eyes still. That intensity that burned for her. And she felt like she was burning up with the desire coursing through her. "Fletcher…"

She reached for him, but he gently pushed her back on the bed. Then he covered her in kisses, from her lips, over her throat and collarbone. He kissed both breasts and flicked his tongue across the nipples.

And she writhed against the bed as the pressure built

inside her. She pulled at his clothes, dragging off his T-shirt, undoing his button and lowering his zipper.

He eased back then, pulled off the last of his clothes and pulled out a condom packet. She took it from him, tore it open with her teeth, then eased the latex over his shaft, running her hand up and down the length of it.

He groaned. "Kiki…"

She pushed him onto his bed and straddled him, easing him inside her. She wanted him so badly. Needed him so badly.

They moved together like they were dancing, in perfect sync, and they even came together, screaming each other's names. She collapsed onto his chest, panting for breath, her heart hammering against his.

He held her close, his arms wrapped tightly around her like he never intended to let her go.

She lifted her face to stare into his, which was tense and serious despite the pleasure they'd just given each other. "What's wrong?" she asked him.

"Nothing," he told her. "I just hope you didn't misunderstand me."

She tensed now and eased away from him. "What do you mean?" Had she read the situation wrong?

"I don't want you to give up your career, Kiki," he said. "You're too talented and you bring people so much happiness and joy. I can't be selfish. I know I have to share you with the world—that you're going to be a star."

Only Grandpa had ever believed and supported her that much. Tears stung her eyes and she blinked furiously.

He touched her face. "Kiki, what's wrong?"

She shook her head. "Nothing. I just love you so much."

"I love you," he said.

She had no doubt. Not about his love or about their future. They would figure out how to make forever work.

* * * * *

#2271 COLTON'S SECRET STALKER
The Coltons of Owl Creek
by Kimberly Van Meter

When Frannie Colton meets mysterious Italian Dante Sinclair in her bookstore, neither can deny their instant attraction. She has no idea Dante is lying about his identity. But when Dante's past catches up with him, it comes for Frannie, too...

#2272 DEADLY MOUNTAIN RESCUE
Sierra's Web • by Tara Taylor Quinn

Police officer Stacy Waltz and her partner, Jesse "Mac" MacDonald, are known all over the state as the ultimate dream team. Then Stacy is targeted by a stalker. Will Mac put his life—and heart—on the line for the colleague who has become so much more?

#2273 HUNTED HOTSHOT HERO
Hotshot Heroes • by Lisa Childs

Hotshot firefighter Rory VanDam is on high alert—and not just from the saboteur targeting his team. Brittany Townsend is an ambitious reporter determined to uncover the truth about him, but what happens when her big scoop leads to a world of danger and desire?

#2274 UNDERCOVER COWBOY PROTECTOR
The Secrets of Hidden Creek Ranch
by Kacy Cross

Navy SEAL turned bodyguard Ace Madden has one mission: protect Sophia Lang. Working undercover as a ranch hand gives him full access to the workaholic executive. But when peril and passion collide, Ace's job becomes personal.

Get 3 FREE REWARDS!

We'll send you 2 FREE Books **plus** a FREE Mystery Gift.

FREE Value Over **$20**

Both the **Harlequin Intrigue** and **Harlequin** Romantic Suspense series feature compelling novels filled with heart-racing action-packed romance that will keep you on the edge of your seat.